# COWBOYS AND VAMPIRES

## VENOM VALLEY

### BOOK ONE

HANK EDWARDS

MITTEN GINGER MEDIA

# SUMMARY

*A small Western town quietly invaded, the residents bitten and turned in the night.*
*A young man finally coming to terms with the immense and unusual power he wields.*
*A friendship tested and evolving into something deeper.*

Vampires are taking over the frontier town of Belkin's Pass, led by an ancient and evil vampire named Balthazar. No one has recognized the evil taking root... until tonight.

Josh Stanton is a wanted man. He's lived on the outskirts of the town's social circles all his life, and, after a tragedy caused by his own hand, flees into Venom Valley, feeling he has no one to turn to for help. Not even Dex, his best friend and a man he secretly loves.

Dex Wells has loved Josh for longer than he can remember. But as a town deputy, he's torn between his feelings for Josh and his duty to the town. When Josh is in trouble, Dex races to Josh's aid ahead of the Sheriff, needing to hear the truth about his situation... and perhaps confess the depth of his feelings.

Glory, a half White, half Apache saloon girl, and the only survivor from the nighttime attack on the One-Eyed Rooster, strikes out on her own. She has no plan, yet, but vows to avenge those she's left behind.

Together, these three unlikely heroes must come together to fight back against the vampire Balthazar. If they fail, his evil will spread across the West and, eventually, the rest of the country.

# CONTENTS

# CHAPTER
# ONE

There was a body inside the house, Josh could feel it.

He stood on the porch as the chill wind blew sand around his boots and against the wood planks of the house. The warming inside him, long absent, had started again. It sat low in his belly, just above his groin, a ball of heat like a stone pulled from the ashes of a smoking fire. It wasn't too bad, not yet, but Josh knew what it meant. He had only felt it twice before, and both times he had been near a dead body.

A dead body that suddenly started to move.

Behind him, Clementine tossed her head and snorted where she stood tied to the porch railing.

"Easy, girl," Josh whispered. He licked his dry lips and reached for the door latch. The warmth spread, became a hot, prickling sensation that filled his chest and spread down his arms, bringing his hand to a stop.

He swallowed the little spit left in his mouth and stared at the door latch. If Agnes were behind the door, he didn't think he could do what had to be done. Not to her. She was the only mother he had known. He should just turn, step off the porch, climb into the saddle, and ride off into the September dusk.

But what if it wasn't Agnes dead inside the house? What if it was someone else, maybe an Indian attacker Agnes had shot before she'd fled to get help? Or an older lady caller who had a bad heart? Josh had to know for sure.

He crossed the porch away from the door in three long strides. His boots sounded hard against the boards of the porch. He leaned his rifle against the house and cupped his hands around his eyes to peer through the dust-streaked window.

A single oil lamp was lit, the flame fluttering in the drafty sitting room. Josh squinted and looked all around the room, but saw no sign of a body.

Yet the heat remained. Banking inside him, growing hotter still. It was as if his blood was being boiled over a fire and poured back inside him.

Clementine snorted again, impatiently it seemed to Josh, and he shot the mare a dirty look. "Clem, hush now. I'll take the saddle off soon."

Josh picked up his rifle and moved back to the door. He adjusted his grip on the wooden stock, checked to make sure the safety was off, then thumbed the door latch and pushed inside.

Shadows filled the long sitting room. They shifted and swayed in the flicker of the lamp. Embers glowed inside the stone fireplace, a sure sign something was amiss: Agnes never let the fire burn down that low during the day. The small dining room was darker still, place settings on the table.

"Agnes?" Josh called and winced at the tremor in his voice. He could feel oily beads of sweat on his forehead and swiped his coat sleeve across the surface.

*Just like a few days ago, out at the Overbrooke farm.*

Josh shook the thought from his mind and headed toward the dining room, intending to check the small bedroom where Agnes slept.

"Agnes? Are you here?"

Blue material on the floor across the sitting room caught the corner of his eye and he stopped fast. A cold spot seemed to bloom inside his chest, a nugget of ice within the waves of heat rolling through him, and he reached up to remove his hat.

"Agnes?"

No response. Agnes lay face down, right hand extended above her head. Her silver hair had come loose from the customary bun and covered her face.

"No, Agnes," Josh said, his voice quiet, almost lost in the sound of the wind. "Not you, too."

As the sun edged lower in the sky, Josh moved to kneel beside her, careful not to get too close. There was no sign of violence that he could see; she must have just fallen where she stood. Her heart, maybe, or that cough she'd had for a while now, which seemed to be getting deeper of late. Whatever it had been, she was gone, and Josh bowed his head. He said a quiet prayer, wishing peace to headstrong, loving Agnes. She had opened her house and her heart to him so many years ago. Stood up against the other townsfolk who called to cast him out even though he'd only been a boy. Streams of sweat mixed with his tears as the heat slowly burned inside him.

Finally, Josh stood and stumbled backward across the room. He was lightheaded and drenched in sweat, the strange heat growing, prickling just beneath his skin. The backs of his legs struck the rocking chair, Agnes's rocking chair, and he sat down hard, the rifle clapping loud against the armrests and making him jump.

He sat and caught his breath as darkness devoured the room. Josh sat stiff and alert in the rocker, resigned to keep watch. He wanted—no, *needed*—to see if the warm feeling inside him meant what it had before. And if it did, he thought he knew how to make sure Agnes stayed dead.

The wind moaned around the house, rattling the windowpanes and throwing sand against the outer walls. It pushed the sand through the gap beneath the door and jiggled the oily flame of the lamp. Josh remained in the rocking chair, hands clutching the wooden arms worn as smooth as Agnes's prized china, while the runners crunched over bits of blown sand. His hat sat on the table beside him, but his rifle lay across his lap. The fluttering lamp was the only light in the room and its jumping flame made his slowly rocking shadow dance across the far wall.

While Josh waited, he thought back on his life with Agnes. She was the town's schoolteacher, unmarried and childless, and she'd heard from folks in the mercantile about the disappearance of Josh's mother from her homestead outside of town. Agnes had left her purchases at the counter and marched into the sheriff's office, her jaw set and eyes hard. When she had left the sheriff's not long after, Josh was by her side, sniffling, scared, and holding tight to her hand.

His mother was never heard from again, but Josh had found a good home.

Agnes had taught him to read and write, to work with numbers, and how to shoot. She had told him to call her Mrs. Pritchett in the classroom, and Agnes at home, and, without a man living under their roof, she had taught Josh how to be one. Probably better than any man in town ever could.

The wind gusted against the house, bringing Josh back to the sitting room. The heat within him continued to climb; it wouldn't be long now. He felt the same way he had a few days ago out at Wayland Overbrooke's farm.

A shudder rippled through him. He could see again the fingers stretching out, clutching at him; could smell the fetid stench of the thing and hear the insistent moan and shuffle of the creature that had once been Wayland Overbrooke. Josh's blood had seemed to burn beneath his skin when he had found Wayland inside the barn, and now, sitting here with Agnes, he once more felt that peculiar heat flowing through him like fire, building steadily into an outright burn.

And when it started to burn, he thought, that's when it would happen.

Sweat slid down his face, and just as he thought it wouldn't be much longer, a soft sound from across the room stopped his rocking. His heartbeat intensified, thumping hard inside his chest as if it wanted to break right through his ribs. Sweat slicked his entire body as the strange heat coursed through him, liquid fire that terrified him and made him feel powerful all at once. He dried his sweaty palms on his breeches and gripped the rifle, narrowing his eyes toward the shadowy corner of the room where Agnes lay.

Had her right hand just twitched?

The sound came again: a quiet scratching-rustle. As Josh watched, a shadow along her skirt shifted and his stomach knotted tighter. His breaths shortened and he couldn't seem to get enough air in his lungs.

When Agnes's foot jumped, he jumped as well. The fingers of her right hand clutched and released, and he watched, wide-eyed and trembling despite the heat washing through him, as her body twitched and shuddered.

Feeling sick to his stomach, Josh turned his head away. He locked his gaze on his hat resting on the table beside him. Agnes had bought him the hat for his fourteenth birthday and he had worn it every day since. She had told him she bought the brown because it matched the color of his eyes.

Another sound from across the room, heavy and sharp, made him jump. It sounded as if Agnes had suddenly slapped her hand down hard against the floor. Josh was determined not to watch; he could not bear to witness Agnes's awful rebirth. He squeezed his eyes shut and tried to recall good times he'd had with Agnes, but the only thing he could remember was the feel of her hand on his, dry and soft, as she taught him the proper way to hold a rifle and pull the trigger.

A moan from Agnes, low and hideous, made his testicles pull up. Josh gasped in a breath and glanced across the room.

Agnes sat upright, her legs stuck out before her, hair hanging loose around her shoulders. Strings of saliva hung from her open mouth, and her hands rested palms up on the floor at her sides, fingers slowly curling in and releasing. The strange heat increased within him, flowing through his body as if he had stepped into a harvest bonfire.

Tears flooded his eyes and a sob surprised him, slipping past his lips before he had the chance to quash it. The thing across the room heard and snapped its head toward him, slinging saliva onto the rug. Josh gasped as his gaze was captured by the thing's eyes, their color a cloudy shade of Agnes's piercing blue.

It moaned, a hungry, angry sound, and Josh had to force himself to remain in the chair, fingers clutching tight to the rifle. Unable to tear his gaze away, he watched as the thing clawed at the rug, its stiffening limbs cracking and popping with its efforts to gain its feet.

Josh pressed his lips tight as he watched it grunt and moan in its struggle to find balance. First, it managed to get on its knees: an abomination of God appearing to pray. It tottered a bit and reached out to keep itself upright, clutching Agnes's beloved side table, nails gouging into the wood. Books tumbled to the floor, covers spilling open to reveal the pages inside. The creature that had once been Agnes, the woman who had loved books and instilled in Josh a love of reading, moved one foot out and stomped down on the book before it. Josh jumped at the awful, heavy sound of its foot coming down. The book proved difficult to stand on and the thing fought for balance, the pages beneath its shoe tearing from the force of its struggles as the side table thumped and skittered against the floor.

The thing across the room finally managed to find its balance. The books it had knocked from the table lay in tatters at its feet. Bright white gashes marred the surface of the side table she had lovingly polished so often over the years. Agnes stood, long skirt twisted around her legs, blouse torn in several places to reveal pale skin beneath. Her head hung down, chin against her chest, and her silver hair a long curtain that hid her face from his view.

Until the thing slowly turned its head and locked its cold, dead gaze on him.

Nothing of Agnes remained. Josh swallowed hard, feeling as if a large, hot stone had been stuffed in his throat. The fire burned fierce now, and sweat coursed down his body. His fingers fumbled with the rifle, working to cock it, his eyes locked on the thing as it turned and took a lurching, unsteady step toward him. Hands that had soothed his forehead when he had been sick with fever and held wet cloths to his skinned knees curled now into claws, eager to tear into him.

Josh double-checked to make sure the rifle's safety was off and that he had chambered a shell, then dried his palms on his breeches again. He took several deep breaths, watching as the thing lurched closer, its hands reaching out, fingers stiff, dirty nails ready to gouge his flesh. It was halfway across the room. Another five staggering steps and it would be upon him.

He stood and raised the rifle to take aim. His hands shook as the thing moved closer, its foot stomping hard against the floor. He licked his lips and dried his eyes on his sleeve. The lamp flame flickered again, slinging shadows around the room and across Agnes's chest.

As it approached, its steps became more certain. It was learning to walk again, and fast.

Josh blinked and thought back to Agnes's lessons on shooting. He could almost feel her standing behind him, arms around his shoulders, lips close to his ear as she said, "Don't pull the trigger. Squeeze it. Slow and steady."

"I'm sorry," he whispered and squeezed the trigger. The rifle bucked in his hand and the flash lit the room, burning an image of Agnes's cruel, hungry face on his mind.

The thing jerked back, a dark hole blossoming on the blouse covering its left shoulder. It took a step back, seemed to hesitate a moment, then moved toward him again.

Josh cocked the gun and moved around behind the chair, raising the rifle to his shoulder. His vision blurred and a tear slid down his cheek, forcing him to dry his eyes on his sleeve.

He shot her again and let out a frustrated, horrified gasp as the bullet tore into her throat. Her head snapped back and she staggered a few steps, hands reaching up to cover the black hole in her skin. Josh could see her jaw working as if she were trying to swallow the lead, then she lifted her head and pinned her cold, dead eyes on him.

"Agnes," he said, his voice high-pitched and strained in the room. "You gotta stay dead. You would not want to live like this."

He worked the lever of the rifle and, even as his blood practically boiled beneath his skin, a cold clutch of fear gripped his stomach when the lever froze in the open position. Jammed.

"Shit," he hissed and looked down at the weapon. He struggled with it, sweat running off his nose and dripping onto the rifle, leaving dark marks on the wood stock.

Cold fingers gripped his arm and he screamed. Jerking his head up, he found Agnes reaching over the rocking chair, the back of it bouncing between them and keeping her from getting a good purchase. Her mouth stretched wide, saliva spilling over her lower lip, teeth glowing in the lamplight.

Josh jerked his arm free and the thing staggered, unbalanced by his sudden movement and the rocking chair. It looked down at the chair a moment and Josh could almost see it thinking, figuring out this was the thing that kept them apart. It pushed the rocker aside and reached for him again, eyes shadowed now with the lamp behind it.

He stepped away, his back coming up against the wall, and realized he was cornered. It had trapped him.

His fingers continued to work the jammed lever as the thing advanced. It dug cold, cruel fingers into his shoulders and leaned in, mouth wide. He braced himself against the wall and kicked it hard in the stomach. The thing staggered back, nails tearing through his shirt and digging furrows into his skin.

Josh cried out and jerked on the lever again. It moved this time and he felt the shell seat itself before the lever closed.

It was coming for him, fingers clutching for purchase.

He lifted the rifle to his shoulder, closed one eye, lined up the sight on the middle of the thing's forehead, and squeezed the trigger.

It fell back, feet going out from under it as it went down hard and flat on its back. The lamp wobbled on the table, oil sloshing in the glass, throwing light around the room in crazy arcs.

Josh moved fast and dropped the rifle, kneeling by the table to grab the lamp before it could fall to the floor and break. He stayed there a moment, catching his breath and waiting for his heart to slow. His blood was cooling, definite proof that the heat was related to the restless dead, and he shivered as his sweat dried in the chill air. His gaze went to where Agnes lay a few feet away, her body still, head turned away, the back of her skull a glistening, gory mess tangled within her silver hair. Just like Wayland Overbrooke, Agnes had needed a bullet in the head to go down.

He picked up his rifle and got to his feet. Moving carefully, he rounded her body and used the barrel of the rifle to move aside her hair. Dead, milky eyes stared at his boots, mouth stretched wide. A neat, round hole marred her forehead, slightly off center.

Josh felt his lip tremble and he turned away as tears flooded his eyes. A single sob tore from his throat, and he dropped to one knee. He covered his eyes with one hand but continued to clutch the rifle in the other. His body trembled, even his insides, as if he would never be warm again.

A sound outside the window brought him back and he jerked his head up. The pale shape of a face hovered behind the glass, almond eyes wide and mouth round with shock. It was Ling Chen, the young Oriental girl Agnes had been instructing in English.

Ling's eyes shifted between Agnes's body and Josh's face.

Josh looked at Agnes, the rifle in his hand, then back to Ling. In a moment of horrifying clarity, he understood how it must look.

"Ling," Josh croaked and rose to his feet, looking up at the window again.

Ling was gone. Josh stumbled to the door, stepping out into the wind-driven night and squinting against the onslaught of sand. All he saw was the rear end of a horse galloping down the road, Ling hunched low and snapping the reins hard, rushing toward town and the sheriff's office.

"No, no, no, no," Josh moaned. He spun in place a moment, looking between the fleeing girl and the inside of the house. What could he do? Ling had seen him by the body, possibly seen him shoot Agnes. Even if he could bury her body, there would be questions and accusations. He would be thrown in jail, and at some point someone would miss Wayland Overbrooke and ride out to his farm.

"Fuck!" he shouted into the furious wind of the night.

He hurried into the house and slammed the door, leaning back against it as he swept his gaze around the small rooms. He had been raised in this house, had spent hours by the fire with Agnes. How could he leave her like this, with no explanation, no respects paid?

But who would believe him?

Dex, maybe. But Dex was just a deputy. The rest of the town would believe what they wanted, even from a Chinese girl. He had to run.

Keeping his gaze averted from Agnes's body, Josh moved through the house. He grabbed clothes, some dried meat and bread. Crouching before the bookcase, he selected a few favorite books and stuffed them in his pack. Agnes had not only encouraged his reading, she had insisted time each day be devoted to it. He would not let her down now.

Picking up his hat, Josh turned to throw a final look at the body consumed by shadows.

"Rest in peace, Agnes," he whispered, his voice breaking on her name. "I will always be grateful for you."

He left the house and pulled the door firmly closed behind him. Clementine stamped and snorted as he mounted her. Josh patted the side of her neck and leaned down to whisper in her ear.

"It's just us now, Clem."

He sat up and clicked his tongue as he pulled the reins. Clementine turned and he urged her into a gallop, heading for the Overbrooke farm. He needed to try and find a connection between the farmer and Agnes. Then he planned to travel farther outside of town to the house where he had once lived with his mother. It stood, vacant and decaying, on the edge of the brutal stretch of desert land known by those in Belkin's Pass as Venom Valley. He would be safe there for a day, maybe two. Perhaps something of his mother's still lay waiting inside the house that might help explain what happened when he got close to the dead.

# TWO

Dex Wells stood beneath the overhang of the boardwalk and leaned against a post. Behind him, the sheriff's office waited, the room lit by a flickering lantern on the desk. The cells beyond the lantern were empty. For now. A hand rolled cigarette jutted out from his lip, the tip glowing orange in the night. Gusts of wind tugged at the cigarette, but he kept the end clamped between his teeth, sucking in the smoke and letting it seep out of his nostrils.

The windows of the One-Eyed Rooster glowed across the dust driven road, and the wind carried the sound of a piano to him. The playing was hard and uneven: Rusty again. The man was an indelicate entertainer, but Sally liked him. She fucked him, most likely, and gave Rusty more playing time than Harry, who Dex preferred. Laughter, some drunken singing, and the surprised squeal of a saloon girl spilled out of the Rooster along with the light. Just another night in Belkin's Pass. Soon the fights would break out, disagreements over a card game or a girl, and he'd wade into the crowd and wait for the fighters to tire themselves out before dragging them across the road and tossing them in the cells.

A strong breath of wind slid over him, pressing on his groin like a lover's cold hand and making his cock stir. As usual when he hardened, he thought of Josh Stanton, then tried to push those thoughts aside. Josh was a friend, that was it, though he hadn't seen Josh for several days now, which was a bit unusual. If he were going to be away for any length of time, maybe helping drive someone's cattle or traveling to another town to pick up something for Agnes, Josh usually let Dex know about it. They'd met in the schoolhouse when they were both boys, and they'd become fast friends. But friends was all Dex thought they could ever be.

He drew smoke into his lungs, savoring the burn in the back of his throat as he narrowed his eyes against the wind. Now that he had realized he hadn't seen Josh for a good spell, he hoped everything was all right with him and Agnes. Tomorrow when he had some time, he'd ride over to the house and check on them. Just a friendly visit, nothing more. They were friends, and that was that. Dex had no doubt Josh would never feel more than a close friendship for him. In all the years they'd known each other, Dex hadn't once felt that Josh saw him as anything more. And, besides, Josh was far smarter than him. He wouldn't want to be held down by a simple deputy. Agnes had poured all her work and hope into him. She had taught the rest of her students well, no doubt about it, but Josh had lived under her roof. He was her only chance at leaving behind a legacy, so Agnes had stayed on the boy to learn as much as he could. And Josh had done just that.

Dex thought about the years he and Josh had spent together, how he had watched over him when Josh had first arrived at the small schoolhouse. As they'd grown up together, their friendship had deepened. Even as the other children avoided Josh, encouraged by their parents who were spooked by the mystery of Josh's mother's disappearance, Dex never once turned his back on him.

When Josh had finally confided in Dex about his mother, relating his hazy memories with a haunted look in his eyes, it had taken all of Dex's willpower not to pull Josh to him and hold him tight. Dex, in turn, had told Josh about his own father's disappearance when Dex had been eight. His father had ridden off to drive their cattle herd down from the grassy pastures in the low mountains that bordered Venom Valley and never returned. Dex's father, his horse, and half the cattle were gone, leaving behind no trace.

The shared loss of a parent had brought the two even closer, and their friendship had deepened. Dex had forced his urges toward Josh deep down inside, tucked safely away. Above all else, he'd not wanted to lose Josh's friendship because of his sinful thoughts. Instead, he thought of Josh when he pleasured himself as he lay in the narrow bed in his small, rented room, the only place his mother had been able to afford for them to live after his father vanished.

Dex now lived in a small rooming house at the edge of town, and when he took himself in hand, as he did most nights, thoughts of Josh still burned in his mind. He remembered the quick glimpses he had managed of Josh when they swam in the river: his hairy balls, the swing of his pale cock beneath the wild blond bush.

As he clasped himself tighter, Dex would imagine what it would be like to kiss Josh: feel the brush of Josh's lips, the damp heat of his breath. He longed to run his tongue down the sun-browned skin of Josh's neck and taste his sweat as Josh sighed and shifted beneath him.

Moving lower, Dex would take Josh's hard length into his mouth, bury his nose in that blond bush and breathe in the smell of sweat. With one hand cupping Josh's balls, he would suck Josh's cock fast, eager for the taste of his seed, wanting nothing more than to swallow it, know the taste and smell of it, of him.

He wanted to know Josh more intimately than anyone else, to lift Josh's legs, feel the weight of the man's calves draped over his shoulders. He wanted to lean down and kiss him, push his tongue between Josh's lips as he pressed the aching length of his cock into Josh's ass.

The heavy stink of his own sweat would fill Dex's nose as he lay in his bed, and he would fight to keep quiet the huff of his breath as his strokes quickened toward climax.

Dex had never been with anyone, man or woman, though many of the saloon girls at the One-Eyed Rooster had tried. He wanted his first time lying with someone to be with Josh, feel the man's sweat-slick skin against his own, taste Josh's tongue in his mouth, feel the hard line of Josh's cock pressing against his belly, the hot grasp of his back passage as Dex pumped into him, slow at first, but steadily quickening.

The sound of a horse disrupted his thoughts, and he shifted to hide his condition, turning to squint up the road. Not many folk were out on such a windy night. Most who had ventured out were already drinking it up at the Rooster. As his cock softened, Dex pulled in another lungful of smoke and watched the horse and rider come into view. It was a young girl, he could tell that right away, hunched low against the wind, reins held tight in her small hands, straight dark hair blown back from her oval face.

As she closed the distance between them, he recognized her: Ling Chen, the young Chinese girl whose father worked the railroad line a few miles outside of town and whose mother washed clothes for unmarried men. Ling drove her horse fast, her expression strained. She was either angry or scared, maybe both. Dex had dealt with the Chens in the past and found them to be a quick-tempered family prone to falling back on their native language when upset. He felt a flash of impatience at the anticipated conversation with Ling, especially because she had interrupted his thoughts of Josh. But he was a lawman, and sworn to help those in need, and by the way Ling was riding, something had spooked her.

Dex flicked his cigarette into the dirt, pulled his hat down tight, and stepped off the boardwalk. Sand and rock crunched beneath his boots as he moved into the road. He raised his hand, turning his body so the light from the One-Eyed Rooster would show the deputy star on his chest.

Ling started at the sight of him, but then recognition flashed across her face, followed closely by relief. She reined in her horse, too hard for how fast she had been pushing it, and the animal reared up.

"Ho! Easy there!" Dex said, keeping his voice firm but calm. He reached for the reins and spoke slowly and calmly, not wanting to spook the horse any further.

Ling stayed on, a testament to her riding skills, and the horse came back to all four hooves. It blew foam and tossed its head as Dex patted the animal's neck and offered his hand to help Ling slide out of the saddle.

She started talking immediately, her words running together, Chinese mixed with English. Her voice was high and strained as she whirled to gesture wildly back the way she had come. When she turned away from him, the wind took her voice completely away. Her eyes were wide as she rattled off words Dex could not understand.

He finally held up a hand and said in the same firm, calm voice he had used on her horse, "Ling!"

Ling snapped her mouth closed and stood blinking at him. The wind blew her hair back from her face and Dex realized that the girl was, in her own way, very pretty.

He took the horse's reins and gestured toward the sheriff's office. "Let's go inside. I'll get you something to help calm you down and you can tell me what happened."

The girl nodded and Dex tied her horse to the rail near the water trough, then preceded Ling into the sheriff's office where he hung his hat on a peg by the door. He sat at his desk and pulled a bottle of rye from a desk drawer. Pouring a small amount into a tin cup, he passed it to Ling who held it in both hands, the cup shaking a bit, and looked up at him.

"Go ahead, it ain't much," Dex assured her. "Just enough to calm you down and warm you up."

Ling raised the cup and sipped the rye. She made a face and coughed, slapping one hand over her mouth as she held the cup out to him in the other. Her eyes watered and she coughed harder, but color came up in her cheeks and her hands stopped shaking.

Once the girl recovered her breath, Dex asked her in a calm, even tone of voice, "You okay now?"

Ling gave several quick nods and licked her lips. "Agnes Pritchett shot."

Dex's stomach twisted hard on itself and a cold seed of dread took root in his chest.

"Agnes Pritchett is dead?" He leaned closer over the desk, hands clasped tight together.

Ling nodded and widened her eyes. "Dead, yes. Shot."

"What about Josh?" he demanded.

Ling nodded fiercely. "Josh! Yes, Josh! He shot."

A panicked anguish sprang from the cold seed in his chest and his mouth went dry. The room seemed to spin around him and he sat back in his chair, grabbing the edge of the desk to steady himself.

"Josh was shot, too?"

Ling frowned, shook her head. "No. He not shot. He shoot her."

The chair creaked beneath his large frame as he leaned forward, relief and disbelief warring inside his heart. "What did you say?"

Ling blinked and leaned back in her chair, looking scared. Her mouth opened, then closed, and she looked around the room as if suddenly aware they were alone. He could imagine her fear: she was a Chinese immigrant accusing a white man who had lived in this town his entire life of murder.

"Ling," he said, pulling back and speaking in as calm and quiet a voice as he could manage, striving to keep the anxiety and anger from coming through in his words. "Tell me again who shot Agnes Pritchett?"

She took a breath and clasped her hands tight in her lap. "Son. Josh."

Dex closed his eyes as a memory of Josh rose unbidden in his mind. Two years ago, after the snowmelt, they had gone to the river for a swim. Dex had caught stealthy glimpses of Josh's body, and the man's pale beauty had stolen his breath. Now, Ling was accusing him of murdering the woman Josh had come to think of as his mother.

Sitting forward again, Dex said, "You saw Josh Stanton shoot Agnes Pritchett?"

Ling nodded. "Shoot, yes. Josh shoot Agnes." She pointed to her forehead. "Here."

Dex stood suddenly, his chair toppling over behind him, hands fisted on the desk. "Where?"

Ling pointed back the way she had come. "Agnes house. Yes."

Clenching his jaw, Dex strode to the door, his boot heels making hard sounds on the wood floor. "Stay here," he said over his shoulder and grabbed his hat from the peg before stepping out into the wind-driven night. The music and laughter from the One-Eyed Rooster seemed to mock his mood as he rode his horse down the road.

When he reached Agnes's house, Dex could see through the sitting room window from his position astride Night-shade. He had been inside the house countless times over the years and knew the layout of every room as if he lived there himself. He could see in the light of the single burning lamp that the rocking chair and side table were out of position, but shadows hid much of the room. Nightshade shifted nervously beneath him and he patted the horse's neck then slid to the ground.

The porch boards creaked beneath his boots and he drew his gun as he released the latch on the door and stepped inside. He could smell the oil from the lamp, Agnes's lavender sachet, and gunpowder. The wind followed him in through the door and the lamp flame danced, making the room's shadows whirl. He closed the door behind him and stepped around the rocking chair then stopped dead as a cold shiver of fear ran up his back.

Agnes lay on her back on the floor, her hair loose, spread around her head like a halo. Her head was turned, eyes open and staring at his boots, her mouth stretched wide. A dark, round hole sat off center in her forehead.

"Dear God," Dex said. He removed his hat and lowered his head a moment in respect. Taking the lamp, he moved through the other two rooms, calling, "Josh? It's Dex. Are you here?"

The house was empty and he returned to the parlor. Kneeling beside Agnes, he set the lantern on the floor near her head and looked her over. He put aside all his memories of Agnes: the many years she had taught him in the schoolhouse, her ease with guns, her skill at poker. Instead, he focused on what the body before him had to say.

From what he could see, she had been shot three times: the shoulder, the neck, and the forehead. The exit wound on the back of her head was a mess of red, gray, and white. Dex looked away, his gaze landing on the bookcase filled with Josh's books. Josh loved Agnes, there was no way he had killed her. But someone had, and Dex would find out who and why they shot her three times.

The wind moaned around the house and Dex shivered at the sound. He looked out the window at the stars stuck in the black quilt of the sky and wondered where he would find Josh.

# THREE

The smoke and heat gathered in the rafters near where Glory leaned on the second floor railing of the One-Eyed Rooster. She breathed it in, all of it, even the noise of the men and the piano, and let it fuel her hunger. Glory felt the itch again and knew she had to do something about it tonight. It might cost her the tiny room at the Rooster, but she'd find something else. She always did.

"Glory!" a girl shouted from the main floor of the saloon.

Glory moved her gaze around the faces, mostly male, all hidden beneath beards or thick mustaches, until she saw a thin, pale arm waving to her through the cigarette smoke. It was Edith, of course, waving for Glory to join her in a tight knot of men. Glory narrowed her eyes and looked over the faces of the men pressed tight around Edith. They looked drunk and hard, one wrong word away from a fight.

Just what she was looking for.

Glory waved back and turned for the stairs down to the saloon's main floor. Sally, the owner of the One-Eyed

Rooster and the woman Glory paid for the opportunity to fuck and sleep in her tiny room, brought her up short.

"You ain't lookin' to start trouble, are you, Glory?" Sally asked. She had once been beautiful, everyone could see that, but the years had taken a toll. And the absinthe. Sally was so thin it sometimes hurt Glory to look at her.

She flashed Sally her most innocent smile. "No trouble at all tonight."

"I hope not," Sally said, her words slightly slurred and her eyes glassy. "Things can be hard for a half-breed whore out on her own." Sally waved for her to pass and Glory moved down the steps, trying to keep time with Rusty's piano playing, but the man was so drunk now he couldn't keep a steady rhythm. She'd be surprised if he'd be able to get it up enough to fuck Sally later when the saloon shut down.

When Glory approached the men around Edith, she let her eyes roam over their broad shoulders and thick arms. Her need to see Ohanzee was so strong it felt physical, like a hunger pang. She needed to see him, feel his strong arms around her, feel the heat of him as he surrounded her, eased her loneliness, kept her safe.

And the only way to see him was to start trouble.

Edith's pale arms pushed two blocky men apart and Glory smiled at the sight of her friend's beaming face. Edith was a good friend, but she could not make Glory feel as she did with Ohanzee. No one could make her feel that way. She loved Edith, loved the girl more than she had loved any other flesh and blood person she'd met in her twenty years, so she needed to be careful Edith wasn't injured. She would never forgive herself if Edith were hurt.

Because Ohanzee could not tell the difference between a friend and an enemy: he lived only to protect her.

Edith's arms wrapped around her, pulling Glory into the circle of men as the girl laughed in her ear. "Glory! I'm so glad you're here." Glory felt the wet press of Edith's lips on her cheek as she looked at the faces of the men all around them. All of the men were drunk, of course, most of them smiling as they swayed on their feet, glasses clutched in their rough hands.

But, as Glory usually found in crowds of men, there was one whose eyes shone cold and cruel. Size never mattered. The man might be bigger than the rest, or the smallest of the group, but she could always depend on one man to have a stone for a heart. And Glory found him standing just behind Edith.

"Fellas, this here is my best friend in the world," Edith said and pulled Glory up against her side. "Say hello to Glory."

A chorus of deep, slurred voices called, "'Lo Glory."

Glory felt a smile tip up the corner of her mouth. It was hard not to smile at something like that. She nodded at the eager, lustful faces, but fixed her gaze on the tall man with the mean eyes standing close to Edith's elbow.

"Howdy, fellas," Glory said. "Havin' a good time?"

Rowdy shouts answered her and she and Edith laughed then hugged each other before Glory continued. "Who wants a drink?"

All the men shouted for whiskey and a tired looking girl brought a tray of shots to the group. The liquor was passed around, including shots for Edith and Glory, and everybody drank. Glory felt the whiskey burn down her throat and coil in her stomach like a snake, fueling her edge. She thought about Ohanzee, imagined his handsome face before her, his strong arms around her, and realized she was starting to get wet beneath her layers of petticoats.

As the whiskey burned inside the group of men, they pressed in closer, the tall man with the mean eyes reaching out to grasp Edith's arm. Edith let out a tiny squeak of surprise and Glory eased her away from the man's grip, switching places with Edith in one smooth move.

The man's eyes, small to begin with, narrowed even further, and he leaned in, his breath foul and hot on Glory's face as he growled, "I got plans for that girl."

"Yeah?" Glory kept Edith behind her, hearing the girl talking happily with the men behind Glory, unaware of the sudden tension. "We got an understanding. We watch out for each other."

"Yeah?" The man leaned in even closer. "I'll take ya both then. Got enough come saved up for the two a'ya."

Glory sneered at him. "With all you had to drink tonight, you couldn't get it up for a goat like you usually do."

The man's hand tightened on his glass and it shattered in his grip. Glory didn't wait for him to make a move, she kicked him between the legs, feeling a cold satisfaction as he doubled over. Surprised shouts and the scrape of furniture being shoved aside exploded around them and Glory watched with excited nervousness as the man rose up before her. His fingers, bloodied from the shattered glass, tightened into a fist, and his small eyes glittered in his red, bearded face.

"No!" Sally shouted over the uproar from her place on the balcony. "No fighting! No fighting!"

Glory smiled as the man drew back his fist, his jaw set, eyes narrowed. A drop of blood trembled on the side of his little finger and then released, falling to the floor just before he brought his fist forward.

A flash of warmth encircled Glory, falling over her like a quilt. The pressure of an invisible hand pressed on her forehead, pushing her head back enough so the man's meaty fist hissed through the air an inch in front of her face. The man staggered, his swing pitching him off balance, and, as he tumbled forward, the invisible force moved Glory aside to avoid him. Glory smiled and did not flinch, clutching her arms across her belly as she felt a warm, invisible arm wrap around her. She could smell wood smoke and damp earth and closed her eyes as the tall, mean man crashed into the men behind her. Shouting followed and then the men around her turned on one another. Glasses flew across the room, and Glory felt herself move to avoid them.

Smiling in the middle of it all with her arms around herself and her eyes closed, Glory felt Ohanzee with her. She heard his voice in her head, speaking to her in his native language, the same language her father had taught her before he had been murdered. It was here, only here, surrounded by danger and threats, that she felt safe. Here was where she felt Ohanzee, where she managed to catch a wavering glimpse of his face and body.

She opened her eyes, ignoring the chaos around her as she stared at the space before her. There he was, just inches away, his dark eyes shimmering in front of her. His skin was golden and perfect, and his lips, full and soft, tipped up in a smile as his black hair hung down his back in a ponytail. He was bare-chested, his smooth skin flawless, his nipples hard brown points that mirrored her own. Visible only to her, his purpose was to keep her safe.

Glory parted her lips and leaned toward him, breathing

in his scent so that it filled her head, her world, pushed into her lungs and spread through her body. Ohanzee, her protector, the one man who would never hurt her, who existed only to protect her. Ohanzee would never let her down, never abandon her.

She was a breath away from his lips, could feel the heat of his mouth close to hers, so close, when someone grabbed her arm and pulled her aside. The warmth vanished as she stumbled away. The noise of the bar crashed over her, startling a scream from her lips, and she looked around to find Edith pulling her toward the bar.

"Edith!" Glory shouted over the shouting and cursing around them. "Stop! Stop it!"

"Come on, Glory," Edith screamed back. "You'll be killed!"

"No, it's all right, I..." Glory turned back, flicking her gaze around the mass of fighting men, searching for Ohanzee, his calm, dark eyes and handsome face. But he was gone. He had protected her, and now that she was out of immediate danger, he had left. As usual.

"No," Glory whispered, and a damp chill seeped into her as she saw the damage caused by the fight. She looked up to find Sally glaring down at her from the balcony, bony fingers clutching the railing. Glory dropped her eyes and let Edith pull her to the relative safety behind the bar. A glass shattered the large mirror behind the bar just a few feet away and they both screamed. A moment later, the roar of a shotgun made the men stop, some with fists drawn back, startled eyes turned up toward the balcony.

Glory looked up along with the rest of the crowd. Sally leaned on the railing, a shotgun thicker than both of her arms propped against her hip.

"Any ya'll want a face full of buckshot, keep at it," Sally shouted, her voice high and mean, eyes glittering with cold menace. "The rest of ya, get the fuck out of my saloon."

The men grumbled and cursed as they collected their hats and other items and shuffled out the door into the windy night. Shattered glass, broken tables and chairs, and sprays of playing cards littered the saloon floor. Rusty, the piano player, cautiously poked his head up from behind the upright. The bartender, a young fella named Clyde, shook his head as he returned his own shotgun to its place beneath the bar.

"Oh, Glory," Edith whispered as the last of the men staggered out the door and Sally started down the stairs. "I think you're in trouble."

"Yep," Glory said and lifted her chin as Sally stepped off the bottom riser and made her way through the ruins of her saloon toward the bar, the shotgun bouncing against her leg with each step. Sally moved around the bar, her blue eyes fixed on Glory's face, arm shaking with the effort of holding the shotgun.

Edith took a step toward Sally. "It weren't Glory's fault—"

Sally silenced her with a look and lowered the shotgun to the floor, leaning it against the bar. She stared into Glory's eyes a moment before slapping her hard across the face.

Glory's head rocked back and she raised a hand to her burning cheek as her eye on that side filled with tears. The slap must have surprised even Ohanzee because he hadn't been able to spare her from it.

Sally squared her shoulders and tossed her thinning brown hair over her shoulder. "Clean this shit up. And your rooming fee is tripled."

Sally turned and stalked back to the stairs. Glory's cheek

burned beneath her palm, but she felt Edith slip her small-boned hand into her own and she turned to smile at her friend as a tear coursed down her cheek.

"I'll help you, Glory," Edith said.

"Thanks."

Glory took a breath of the stale beer and liquor-scented air and thought of Ohanzee as she and Edith grabbed brooms from behind the bar. She might be broke for the rest of her life, but it was worth it to see him again, feel his touch, and breathe his scent. Someday she'd figure out a way to keep him with her longer than a few dangerous moments.

# FOUR

Glory awoke with a shudder that seemed to shake her very bones. She'd pulled her knees to her chest in her sleep and her legs ached from the position. With a quiet wince, Glory straightened her legs and turned her head to peer across the narrow room. She squinted hard, trying to penetrate the deep shadows and pale blue moonlight, and her breath stuttered in surprise to find the door to the hall standing open. Glory always closed her door at night; she didn't like the thought of Sally or one of the other girls picking through her stuff while she slept.

"Edith?" Glory said quietly into the darkness. Sometimes the girl got lonely or had a bad dream and crept into Glory's room. "Is that you?"

The dark was silent around her. The rest of the saloon girls were sleeping hard, and Sally was probably filled up with absinthe. But someone was close, she could feel it. Standing just outside the door or moving softly along the hall, peering in the doors of the other girls' rooms.

In a breath, the air in her small room changed. A great

cold fell across her, as if winter had come to just her bedroom. Glory shivered against her thin mattress and curled her fingers into the ends of the scratchy blanket. A form filled the door of her room: tall and wide-shouldered. The moonlight revealed only the bottom half of him, dressed in black breeches and heavy black boots.

"Who are you?" Glory asked in a quiet voice. "You ain't supposed to be here."

The form stood very still and Glory wondered if she were seeing things in the dark. The familiar warmth of Ohanzee surrounded her, chasing away the chill. She was definitely in trouble. But Ohanzee would protect her; he would always protect her. She hadn't yet found a thing that would break his protection, and Lord knew she had tried.

"Get out," she said in a voice as strong as she could manage. Even though she knew Ohanzee was with her, could feel his protection surrounding her, there was something about this strange visitor that frightened her. "You ain't welcome here."

The shape at the door seemed to flicker, as if she was looking at it through a candle flame, and the cold in the room grew stronger, pushing closer around her. She could feel the bite of the air as it found its way through Ohanzee's protection and her heart fluttered as she wondered if maybe this was it. Had something more powerful than Ohanzee finally found her. She had laughed at Death so often he'd gotten mad enough to send an angel of Hell to fetch her soul.

As if reading her thoughts, the figure in the doorway turned its head slightly and where its eyes should be she saw two glowing red orbs. Fear iced all through her as she understood this figure in front of her was no man.

"Let me in." The voice was at once terrifying and soothing.

Before she could even consider a reply, Glory felt Ohanzee's form beside her. It was like it always was, one moment she was on her own and the next he was with her. Always before he had stood before her, his dark eyes fixed on hers, lips pressed together, his cheekbones reflecting the shivery light of his protection. No, not just protection; love. After all these years Glory could tell he loved her. And she loved him; most likely always had.

This time, however, was different. Ohanzee lay alongside her on the mattress. She could feel the length of his body pressed against hers and a deep thrum of longing quivered through her. She had never felt him lie against her before, and it made her ache for him. The most contact she'd had with him before this was last year when he had wrapped his arms around her to protect her from a speeding stagecoach. That time she had felt the sureness of his grip on her, felt his breath against her face and the fleeting press of his lips against hers as the stagecoach had sped past, barely missing her. After all these years, it had taken a speeding stagecoach for him to be able to kiss her.

Now, however, she felt the full length of him burn against her, and even in the depths of her fear of the stranger in her doorway, Glory felt herself respond. She turned her head, eyes wide and staring at the vision of Ohanzee that shimmered beside her within a golden light. His face was turned in profile, his nose like a mountain ridge silhouetted against the moonlight, his dark eyes staring at the figure across the room that Glory had all but forgotten. She could not take her gaze from the sight of Ohanzee there in beside her, stretched out at her side as if they were waking up together as husband and wife.

"It's you," she whispered, "I can't believe you're here. Like this."

The shape in the door fluttered and a low hiss floated across the dark. She pulled her eyes from Ohanzee's face to glance toward the door. The man made a gesture, something sharp and angry, then moved silently away. The cold that had invaded her room seemed to follow behind. Moonlight touched her doorframe again, glazing it in pale light, and she rolled her head to look at Ohanzee. He turned to fix her with his dark eyed gaze. For a moment, no longer than it took her to breathe in and out, they looked at each other, saw each other plainly. Glory could see the desire in his dark eyes, feel the almost-there touch of his hand as it slid beneath her petticoats up her thigh. She had just started to lean toward him, lips parting as she moved in for a kiss and Ohanzee's hand traveled higher. Then, as she watched, he began to fade from view.

"No!" Glory said, her voice a loud snap in the dark, quiet room. She reached for him, tried to touch him one last time, but the glimmer of his golden light faded into the darkness. The touch of his hand on her leg evaporated and the chill of the night air surrounded her again. "No, it's not fair. It's not fair."

Glory pressed her face into the blanket where Ohanzee had lain for a moment and tried to breathe in the smell of him, to draw a part of him into her to keep beside her heart. All she found, however, was prairie dust and the dried sweat of the men she had been with the past weeks. She lay on her side and pushed her face hard into the rough ticking of the mattress, allowing herself a moment to cry. As she wept,

Glory ran her hand over her hip and down her thigh, lifting her petticoat and moving her hand up her thigh. She closed her eyes and thought about Ohanzee, imaging her fingers were his, that he had remained long enough for his hand to reach its goal. His touch would be soft, unhurried. So unlike the other men she'd been with.

Afterward, she eased her grip on the blanket and lowered her spine to the mattress, her right hand slipping down her thigh.

Then she heard a quiet intake of breath and her senses sharpened. She raised her head and squinted toward the door where the dark shape had stood just minutes before. A flush of embarrassment warmed her as she considered the possibility that someone had witnessed her self-pleasure, but she forced that aside. Turning her head slightly, she listened.

Something was wrong in the saloon.

The stranger who had stood in her doorway was still inside the One-Eyed Rooster.

Again Glory heard the quiet, sharp intake of breath. She sat up on the bed, turning to put her bare feet on the cold wooden floor. Her heart seemed to gallop in her chest, but the danger must not be immediate for she could not feel Ohanzee's spirit around her. Yet.

She stood up and made her way to the door, pausing to swallow the fear lodged in her throat before she stepped over the threshold and into the upstairs hall.

The moonlight cast a blue glow along the hallway. The second floor railing was etched in shadow on the wall beside her as she crept from door to door. Her petticoats rustled, a stampede of sound in the quiet, still dark of the saloon, and she clutched them tight against the front of her legs to keep the noise to a minimum. She passed a number of closed doors, hearing the snores of Beatrice behind one and rolling her eyes, thankful their rooms didn't share a wall. Another two rooms down, the moonlight revealed a door standing ajar and her stomach quivered nervously when she realized it was Edith's.

Glory hurried forward, her bare feet whispering across the sandy wooden planks. When she reached Edith's door, she gently pushed it open. Her gaze went to the bed against the wall, and Glory's breath caught in her throat.

Edith sat up on her mattress, her head tipped back to expose the pale skin of her throat. A dark, broad shouldered man sat beside her, thick arms wrapped around Edith's narrow frame, head angled down toward Edith's neck, face turned away. As Glory watched, Edith's hand lying palm up on the thin mattress twitched, the fingers curling in as if wanting to hold in place a whispered secret. Edith's lips parted and she let out a quiet gasp, the same sound that had brought Glory out of her thoughts of Ohanzee and down the hall.

"Hey now!" Glory said in a loud voice, as if speaking to an unsettled animal. "Get away from her."

The man lifted his head, eyes closed, face raised to the ceiling. The moonlight revealed a satisfied look on his face as well as a dark set of whiskers around his mouth and pointed chin. Just as the realization hit her that what she had first thought of as whiskers was, in fact, blood, Glory's stomach trembled and twisted in on itself and the warm glow of Ohanzee's protective spirit burst into life around her.

The stranger lowered his head and opened his eyes. They glowed red in the dark and he looked at her with a smug, cold smile on his face. The skin stretched tight on his skull glowed like pale silk in the moonlight. His smile sent a web of terrified chills across the top of her head and down her back, and even the warm pulse of Ohanzee's spirit around her could not help her feel warm.

"What would you have me do?" the man said, his voice smooth, but tainted with an accent Glory had never heard before. He stood, allowing Edith to fall onto her back against the mattress, two small wounds in her throat oozing blood. Glory's attention had been drawn to Edith, to the blood on her neck and shoulder, and when she shifted her gaze back to the pale man, she was surprised to find him standing less than a foot away. Her heart clutched inside her chest and she drew in a sharp breath of surprise at his nearness. How had he approached her so quietly, so quickly?

His red-eyed gaze darted around her face and slid up and down her body. His brows, heavy and dark above his flaming eyes, drew down. The dark tip of his tongue slipped out and ran along his thin lips, cleaning up the last traces of Edith's blood. Glory shuddered and dropped her gaze to the floor, clutching her hands together in front of her.

"Look at me," the man said, his voice low and smooth, coaxing her to raise her eyes even as the warmth of Ohanzee's protection intensified. She met his gaze, stared into his fierce red eyes, and set her mouth as she pushed out her chin.

He smiled, revealing sharp, pointed teeth that gleamed in the moonlight. "My, you're a stubborn one. And stupidly brave. What is your name?"

"Glory," she said, then cursed herself.

"Glory," the man repeated slowly, playing her name along his tongue and past his lips. "I very much like that name. I am Balthazar, and I am pleased to make your acquaintance."

"Get out of this saloon," Glory demanded. "You're not welcome here."

Balthazar's expression changed to one of surprise, then suddenly he stood behind her, leaning close enough for Glory to feel the cold coming off him. She shivered and sucked in a startled breath, turning her head to keep him in sight but afraid to fully face him.

Balthazar drew in a breath through his nose. Leaning in even closer, he whispered, "I smell the fear rolling off of you like a delicate perfume. But something keeps me from you, some spell or spirit. I must admit, I am intrigued." He laughed, a quiet, chilling chuckle, and Glory took a step forward and away before turning to face him. She could feel the urge to run, to flee back to her own room, slam the door, and wedge a chair beneath the knob. But she had Ohanzee for protection. She could feel him there with her, his arms around her, keeping her safe. And she would not leave Edith to Balthazar's whims.

"You cannot order me from this place," Balthazar said, his voice thick and wet. "For you are not the one who owns it." He stepped closer, head cocked as he studied her face, his red eyes lingering on her neck. "You are fortunate to find me well fed now that you are removed from the safety of your room." He leaned just a bit closer and clicked his sharp teeth together, the sound making her jump. He drew back and laughed again. "Next time, with or without your spirit guide, you may not be so lucky." His eyes shifted over her shoulder and he smiled. "Dear Edith is always delicious, but you smell simply divine."

Glory glanced over to where Edith lay on her back, arms at her side, skin so pale in the moonlight she might be dead. When she turned back, Glory was startled to find Balthazar gone. The cold in the room seeped away as did the warmth of Ohanzee's protection. Glory took a couple of shaky breaths then moved to the bed to take Edith's hand. The girl's skin felt so cold, it was as if Glory had found her under a drift of snow.

"Edith," Glory whispered, and gave the girl a gentle shake. "Come on, love, open your eyes for me. It's Glory, come on, look at me."

Edith made no movement except for the gentle rise and fall of her chest. Glory rubbed Edith's hand to try and warm her, then finally pushed the girl to the other side of the bed and stretched out beside her. She pulled the thin blanket up over both of them and put one arm across Edith's chest and the other beneath her neck in an effort to warm her.

"It's okay, love," Glory assured her in a quiet voice. "He's gone. I won't let him hurt you again, I promise."

But even as she said the words, Glory felt the lie wrapped inside them. She closed her eyes and hugged Edith tighter to her, trading her warmth for the girl's cold and counting the moments until sunrise.

# FIVE

Dex sat on the steps of the boardwalk in front of the sheriff's office and watched the sun rise. As it cleared the distant mountain range, the sun stained the dusty air the color of blood. He took a drag from his cigarette and turned to squint at the shadowed doorway of the One-Eyed Rooster. Sally had kicked all her customers out early last night after a fuss brought on by one of her girls. All those men, full as ticks and still pent up from pawing at saloon girls and not allowed to conduct their business. The fight that had started in the saloon had continued in the street, the men throwing their fists, and Dex had ridden right up on it as he returned from Agnes's house.

It had taken him quite a time to break up the skirmishes, catching a few fists himself as he did. He had been dirty, tired, and angry and ended up throwing more than a dozen men in jail, more out of spite than anything else.

No one in town except Ling and the doc knew yet that Agnes Pritchett was dead, and only Ling knew of Josh's possible involvement. Dex wanted to keep her accusation quiet for as long as he could. Once people heard that Agnes had been murdered, by the man she'd raised as her own son, no less, they'd form a lynching mob and hunt Josh down like a rabid dog without any trial or question. Dex was not about to let that happen. He had a lot of questions for Josh, and he wanted to ask them of the man face to face.

The door to the sheriff's office opened behind him and Dex turned to peer over his shoulder. Albus Brandt, the town doctor, stepped out onto the porch with his hat in his large hands. The man was thin as a rail with an egg shaped head that sported a few stubborn wisps of white hair.

"Damn shame about Agnes," Doc Brandt said.

Dex nodded and dropped his gaze to the wooden step beneath his boots. "Sure is. She was a good woman."

Doc Brandt took a deep breath and released it. "Don't know who'd wanna shoot her, of all people. She never crossed anyone in town."

Dex took a deep drag off his cigarette and stared down at his dusty boots. He wouldn't be able to keep Josh's possible involvement a secret much longer. Once the sheriff returned to town, Ling was bound to tell him what she had told Dex.

He tossed his cigarette into the road and stood up. Every muscle in his body ached with exhaustion. It had been a long, physically demanding night, and all he craved now was a few hours of sleep in his tiny room on the top floor of Beatrice Gallows's house before the sun made it too hot. But sleep would have to wait; he needed to find Josh.

Dex turned to face Doc Brandt and lifted his chin toward the sheriff's office. "How they doin'?"

Doc Brandt glanced over his shoulder, then turned back and made a face as he shook his head. He put on his hat and waved a hand toward the office. "They'll be fine. Just have a headache once they come out from under all that whiskey. Some of 'em'll have bruises, some scrapes." He shook his head again. "Damn fools." He stared at something over Dex's shoulder.

Dex turned and followed Doc Brandt's gaze across the road to the door of the One-Eyed Rooster. The new girl leaned in the doorway, arms crossed, chin stuck out like granite, her dark hair loose and tousled by the wind. She stared back, eyes narrowed. Dex thought her name was Gloria or something like that. She was a half-breed, and she looked like more than a handful for any man to try and tame.

He turned back to Doc Brandt and said in a low voice, "I'd like to keep Agnes's murder quiet for now. Don't want people to talk themselves into a fright with the sheriff out of town."

Doc Brandt bit his lower lip and nodded, his gaze dropping to the boardwalk. "I reckon you've got a point there. But people will start to look for her." He lifted his gaze and squinted at Dex. "Have you seen Josh?"

Dex shook his head. "Not yet. I plan to ride out later and look for him."

Doc Brandt took a step closer and lowered his voice, leaning in to say, "You don't think Josh could have had anything to do with this?"

A hot spike of anger stabbed into his chest, but Dex clenched his fists and shook his head. "I've known Josh since Agnes first adopted him. He loved her and would never do a thing to harm her."

"Well, don't you find it odd he's gone missing around the time you found Agnes's body?" Doc fixed narrowed, suspicious eyes on Dex's face. "He was born out on the edge of town to that woman people claimed practiced witchcraft, you know."

"Yep, and kids in town say his old house is haunted, too. I thought you of all people in this town would know the difference between ghost stories and truth." Dex spat into the dry, dusty dirt and glared the doc back a step. "Seems to me we should be worried about Josh gone missing and not suspicious. Whoever shot Agnes could have taken him for God knows what reason."

Doc grunted and looked away, finally saying after a moment of silence, "What should we tell people if they start looking for Agnes? Or Josh for that matter?"

Dex let out a breath and glanced around, his eyes falling on the girl in the doorway of the One-Eyed Rooster. She still stared at them, eyes hard and flat even at this distance.

"Tell them you haven't seen either of them out and about, that's all."

"All right, but you know how I feel about keeping the truth from people."

Dex turned back to the doctor and nodded. "I know. I hate asking you to do it, but it's best for now."

Doc Brandt hesitated, appeared to be on the verge of saying something more, then finally lifted a hand and turned to walk off along the boardwalk, the rising sun throwing his thin shadow on the walls of the buildings he passed. Dex watched the man amble off, then ran his hands over his face, trying to shake loose the exhaustion that clung to him. He didn't have much time. Sheriff Haden would be back in town come morning, and Dex needed to find out what had happened in Agnes's house. And the only place he might find answers to his questions was with Josh.

"Hello! Deputy Dex!"

Dex winced at the high-pitched voice that hailed him from across the street. He fixed a smile on his unshaven face and turned to watch Eleanor McBriddle make her way across the dirt road. She held her skirt up with one hand, expertly stepping around horse pies as she approached. A broad brimmed hat with ribbons flowing off the back shielded her soft, fleshy face from the sun, and Dex had to stop himself from rolling his eyes. Eleanor McBriddle was married to Langstrom McBriddle, who owned the only mercantile in Belkin's Pass.

"Deputy Dex!" Eleanor panted as she climbed the steps onto the boardwalk. "So glad I caught you. The sheriff is still off visiting his daughter, is he not?"

"That he is, Mrs. McBriddle. Can I help you with something?"

"Well, I suppose so. I've been trying to reach someone for days now."

Dex's stomach twisted nervously. Was he already going to have to start lying about Agnes's fate?

He tried to keep his expression only slightly concerned as he asked, "Oh? And who might that be?"

"Why, Wayland Overbrooke," Eleanor said. "I buy my eggs from him, but he's not come to town in days. I don't know how I'm to make my angel food cake for the social without those eggs."

"Did you go out to his farm?"

Eleanor widened her eyes beneath her hat. "I don't ride that far outside of town, Deputy Dex. What with those redskins out there just lying in wait to take a white woman off into the wilds and do unmentionable things." She crossed her arms and fixed him with a steely look, her thin lips pressed even thinner. "I would like to know where that man is with my eggs, and I would hope you would ride out to his farm and find out."

Dex let out a breath and dropped his gaze to the boardwalk. The Overbrooke farm was on the way out of town, in the same direction as the old house where Josh had once lived with his mother.

He lifted his gaze to Eleanor's pale blue eyes and nodded. "I'll ride out there later this morning and see what I can find out for you, Mrs. McBriddle."

Her face relaxed, the lines softening as her tight lips creased upward in a smile. "Thank you, Deputy Dex. I look forward to receiving your report."

"I'll let you know what I find as soon as I return to town." Dex tipped his hat and Eleanor bowed her head in reply before turning to walk off along the boardwalk.

Dex watched her go a moment then let out a long breath. The sun was barely over the mountain range outside of town and already he was on someone else's mission. He turned and pushed through the door into the sheriff's office and the grumblings of the drunks locked in the cells. He ignored the men and set about making coffee, placing the pot on the stove in the corner.

He would wait for Wallace, the town's other deputy, to come into the office before he set out for the Overbrooke farm and then the old Stanton house far outside the town limits. Wallace was young, too young, in Dex's opinion, to be a deputy, but he'd have to handle releasing the drunks from their cells. Dex could only do so much.

As he waited for the coffee to boil, Dex sat at the desk and put his head in his hands, thinking about Josh. A tiny flutter of doubt stirred deep inside his gut as he thought about Doc Brandt's words: *He was born to a woman people claimed practiced witchcraft, you know.*

Could Josh have shot Agnes like Ling claimed she saw through the window? The girl had been scared, that much Dex had seen for himself. But he could not believe Josh had been the one to shoot Agnes.

And yet—Dex had noticed Josh's rifle, hat, and some books were missing from the house when he had searched it earlier. What if Josh had shot Agnes and was now on the run?

More questions and no answers flooded his mind and Dex turned to pour himself a cup of coffee. All he knew was that he needed to find Josh before anyone else in town found him, and he needed to ask him a lot of questions.

# SIX

Glory watched the deputy, Dex she thought his name was, glance her way one last time before he went into the sheriff's office. The man was tall and handsome with blue eyes that looked a little sad to Glory when she saw him on the odd occasion he would stop in the saloon for a drink. He was kind and quiet, strong when he needed to step in and settle something, and he never took one of the girls upstairs. Glory respected Dex for that. He seemed a good man, and she wished things were different so she could get to know him better. But a sheriff's deputy wasn't about to be seen with the likes of a common saloon girl, and a half-breed girl at that. That kind of thing wasn't proper.

She took a breath, filling her lungs with dusty air, and exhaled before shifting her gaze to the heavy woman making her way off the boardwalk and out onto the street. She didn't know the woman's name, she was higher class than Glory and, like Dex, they would never mix company. As if to reinforce Glory's thought, the woman glanced her way and wrinkled her nose in distaste before lifting her chin and stomping away, the ribbons of her hat flowing behind.

A sigh slipped from Glory's lips before she could think to stop it, and she turned to look around the empty, dusty saloon behind her. Flies buzzed over the darkened wood where she and Edith had wiped up the spilled whiskey and beer. Five of the twelve tables had been smashed in the brawl last night, along with a great number of chairs. Bottles and glasses had been broken over heads and underfoot, and Glory and Edith had been up late sweeping up the shards.

Edith. The memory of finding her friend in the dark man's embrace early that morning gave Glory a chill that shook her sturdy frame. Standing in the reflected glow of the rising sun, Glory had a difficult time believing the man and his threats had been real. Maybe she had dreamed it. But then she thought of Ohanzee, recalled the touch of him as he lay beside her, then pleasuring herself afterward. Something had happened last night, that much she knew. And she had awakened that morning in Edith's bed, the girl stiff and chill beside her, lips pale and eyelids brushed blue.

After a luxurious stretch that earned a whistle from a rider passing in the street, Glory crossed the floor and made her way up the steps. All the girls were still asleep even though they had gone to bed long before Glory and Edith, bored after the men had been forced to leave the saloon hours earlier than usual. At the top of the steps, Glory turned toward Edith's room and eased the door open. Edith lay where Glory had left her, flat on her back, arms at her sides. Her breathing was deep and even, but her face still looked pale in the diffused sunlight coming in through the dusty old drapes.

"Edith, love," Glory whispered as she entered the room.

"Time to get up." She crossed to the window and pulled the drapes apart, letting in a flood of sunlight.

Edith moaned as the light fell across her, the first sound Glory had heard from her since they had gone to bed. The girl lifted a hand in a feeble attempt to block the light and turned her face to the wall, but not before Glory saw the pain in her expression.

"Edith?"

"Glory? That you?" Edith's voice sounded frail and weak.

"It is, it's me."

"The light hurts my eyes," Edith groaned. "Close the drapes?"

Glory pulled the drapes tight, and looked over her shoulder to see Edith roll onto her back again, her face relaxed but still quite pale. She crossed to sit on the edge of the mattress and took Edith's cold hand between hers.

"You're so cold," Glory said. "I think you're coming down sick."

Edith licked dry lips and smiled up at her. "I'm fine. Just tired's all. Stayed up too late helping you clean."

"I know, and I thank you," Glory told her. "I hope you know how much it meant to me. No other girl would have done that."

Edith tightened cold fingers around Glory's hand, lips curling into a smile though her eyes remained closed. "We're friends. That's what friends do."

Glory frowned and laid a hand on Edith's forehead, but her skin was cool and dry. "You got no fever. But you're awfully pale. You stay in bed today, hear? I'll bring you up something to eat in a bit."

"Okay," Edith whispered, her voice nothing more than a breath.

Glory stood and moved toward the door, but Edith called to her and she turned back. "What is it, love?"

"I had the strangest dreams last night," Edith said.

A sudden chill rattled up Glory's spine. "Oh?"

Edith smiled and, to Glory's embarrassment, moved her hand to touch herself through her petticoats. "I dreamed a man came to visit me last night. He was older, and not at all like the men we usually see. He was from far away and he kissed me so nice." Edith's hand pressed hard into her petticoats and Glory felt her cheeks warm with embarrassment. It was almost as if Edith was showing her she knew what Glory herself had done last night.

"Did he tell you his name?" Glory asked.

"He did, but it was strange, like a Bible name, and I've forgot it." Edith lay on her bed in the shadows, eyes closed, fingers touching and pressing herself through her petticoats.

Glory swallowed past the dry lump in her throat. "Was it Balthazar?"

Edith's hand paused and she turned her head toward Glory, opening her eyes and staring at her with surprise. "It was. Oh, Glory, have you met him, too?"

"Yes, but he ain't a good man."

Edith closed her eyes and frowned. "Why do you say that?"

"I just thought he wasn't to be trusted," Glory said. "If he comes back, will you tell him to leave?"

Edith shook her head against the mattress. "No. I like him."

"Edith, please, for me?"

Edith was quiet for a long time. "But I like him."

"I know that, but I think he's lied to you. He ain't a good man. Will you tell him to go?"

Another stretch of silence, so long this time Glory had started to think the girl had fallen to sleep. But then, in a weak voice, Edith whispered, "I'll think about it."

An uncertain relief flooded Glory's chest. "Truly think about it?"

"I will. Please go, I'm tired."

"All right. I'll come back later with something for you to eat."

Glory stepped out into the hall and pulled the door closed. She stood with her head against the frame and listened to the sounds of the town coming in through the door to the street. After several minutes, Glory walked to the next door along the hall. This room was Laura's, a quiet girl with light brown hair, wide blue eyes, and two missing teeth. Glory knocked then let herself into the room darkened by heavy drapes.

She found Laura lying on her back, sleeping hard, her hair half covering her face. Her skin was pale and cool to the touch, the same as Edith's, and touching Laura's skin left a cold spot of dread in Glory's chest.

"Laura?" Glory gave the girl a gentle shake, but she would not waken. "Laura, wake up. Daylight's wastin'." Glory shook Laura harder but still the girl would not awaken. Finally, Glory gave up and left the room, her initial unease growing to fear. What was happening to the girls of the One-Eyed Rooster?

Moving down the hall, Glory found the rest of the girls just as listless and pale as Edith and Laura. By the time she arrived at the last door, Beatrice's room, fear had wedged itself hard in her chest, making it difficult to breathe. She did not bother to knock, she had left behind manners and propriety three rooms ago, and she simply barged in the room.

Beatrice, the girl who snored louder than most of the men Glory had lain with, was a messy lump of a girl. She was, as some delicately put it, of "farm stock", with broad shoulders and wide hips. The men liked her for her adventurous spirit, and it was rumored Beatrice was open to all manner of pleasure, even those things considered taboo by Sally and the other girls.

The drapes in Beatrice's room were drawn, the same as the rooms of all the other girls. Glory could see piles of clothing scattered around the floor and wrinkled her nose at the smell of sweat and unclean garments hanging in the air. Turning, she squinted toward the bed, able to make out the curved shape of Beatrice beneath the blanket.

"Beatrice?" Glory called quietly.

"Go the fuck 'way," came the scratchy-voiced reply.

"You feeling all right?" Glory asked, taking a step toward the bed.

Beatrice lay on her side with her back toward Glory. A stripe of sunlight lay across the girl's back, exposing the loosened strings of her corset and the pale flesh that pushed out over the top of the garment.

"Beatrice?" Glory tried again. "Do you feel ill?"

With a sudden flailing of her arms, Beatrice rolled over and glared at Glory. The full force of Beatrice's anger was clear, even in the dim light of the room, and Glory let out a relieved breath. It was Beatrice all right, full of piss and vinegar just like every other day.

"What the fuck you doing in here?" Beatrice croaked. "Get your twat out of my room."

Glory stepped closer to the bed. "Something's wrong with the other girls."

Beatrice yawned and snorted, flopping onto her back and rubbing her eyes with her thick, blunt fingers. "Just finding that out now, are ya?"

Glory rolled her eyes. "No, something serious. They're all pale and cool to the touch."

Beatrice sat up and swung her big feet over the side of the bed. Her large breasts strained against the corset as she yawned again, then fixed Glory with a bleary, angry eye. "I ain't the fuckin' doctor. Why you tellin' me this?"

"I think someone's done something to them."

Beatrice snorted. "Yeah, and they got paid for it."

"No, I mean someone was in here last night. A man."

Beatrice glared up at Glory. "There are men in here every night, Glory. What the fuck are you on about?"

"Sally threw out all the men early last night, after the fight, remember?"

"Yeah, a fight you started. Thanks for losing us all a night's wages." Beatrice shoved herself up off the bed and started toward her.

Glory took several steps back until she stood in the open doorway, eyes wide as she watched Beatrice stomp closer. The girl placed a hand on Glory's chest between her breasts and pushed her out into the hall. With a final glare, Beatrice slammed the door shut. Glory stood outside Beatrice's door and listened to the girl trod heavily across the room and then the groan of the bed as she collapsed on it again.

Turning, Glory eyed the door of Sally's room at the end of the hall. The fancy glass knob glittered in a sunbeam like a jewel. With a breath to fortify her, Glory marched down the hall, trailing one hand along the second floor railing. Her blood raced, she could feel her heart beat in her temple, and her breath came in short, quick bursts. Sally would know what to do; she wouldn't want anything happening to her girls, her sources of income.

Before Glory could reach the door, the glass knob turned and the heavy wooden door swung slowly inward. Darkness lay thick beyond the threshold, and Glory stopped a dozen steps short, her skin breaking out in gooseflesh. The doorway stood empty a moment, then a small, pale hand curled around the edge of the door, dirt showing beneath her nails. Sally stuck her head out from behind the door and peered at Glory through slitted eyes.

"Who's that?" Sally slurred.

Glory let out a breath. Sally wasn't sick like the other girls; she was just trying to shake off her nightly absinthe.

"Glory."

Sally frowned and ran a hand over her face. "Glory? Thought I fired you last night."

Glory opened her mouth, closed it as she thought a moment, then took a chance. "No, ma'am. Doubled my room fee's all."

"Doubled?" Sally licked her lips. "Sounds fair. Where's Cook?"

Glory glanced down the stairs on her right to the empty saloon. "Haven't seen Cook yet, ma'am. None of the other girls are up yet. I think they may be coming down with something."

Sally sighed, her lips pursing around the sound like a kiss. "Sick? That what you mean?"

"Something like that."

"Well they'd better feel up to workin' tonight since you made us miss a night of payin' customers." Sally glared at

Glory a moment, then waved her away. "Go find Cook and get the breakfast going. I'll be around in a bit."

As Glory walked down the steps, she tallied the numbers in her head: there were six other girls living in the One-Eyed Rooster. Out of those, five were sick like Edith. Only Beatrice, herself, and Sally seemed to have been spared. Something strange was definitely going on. Once she had roused Cook, Glory would try to figure out something she could do. They were all sisters, in a way, and she couldn't let them suffer without trying to help.

# CHAPTER
# SEVEN

The flies had been at Wayland Overbrooke's swollen, gape-mouthed corpse as well as the mangled chickens, and Dex had to turn away from the sight and stench of it. He retreated outside the barn door, breathing deep to keep his breakfast down as a veil of cold sweat dotted his forehead. Two bodies within a day of one another, and Wayland surrounded by mangled chickens. Agnes had died recently, but Dex could tell Wayland had been dead for a few days at least, probably longer. He wondered if the deaths might be connected, taking into account the strange details surrounding each.

And Wayland's farm was on the road that led to the house where Josh had once lived.

With his stomach under control, Dex covered his mouth and nose with his handkerchief. He tied the loose ends behind his head, then walked back into the barn. Stopping just inside the door, Dex let his gaze move around the barn's interior drenched in shadows, trying to understand the details of what had caused Wayland's death.

The eighth rung up the ladder to the hayloft had broken, the splintered ends white around the black, old exterior wood, telling Dex the break had happened recently. At the foot of the ladder, the straw had been flattened in roughly the length of Wayland's body. Dex figured Wayland had fallen either going up or climbing down from the hayloft and lay for a time on the hard dirt floor of the barn. Depending on how he had landed, Wayland could have badly injured himself.

That part made sense, but then Dex noticed more details that made his brows knit together above the ragged end of the handkerchief. The straw around the flattened spot beneath the ladder was disturbed. Wayland had, at some point after falling, stood up. The dead chickens lay scattered about the barn, feathers bloodied, missing chunks of raw flesh. In the middle of the dead chickens lay Wayland, on his back, head canted toward Dex, milky eyes staring at Dex's boots.

Just like Agnes.

And, also like Agnes, Dex now noticed that Wayland appeared to have been shot a number of times, at least once in the forehead.

"Josh," Dex whispered, his breath fluttering the handkerchief. "What's this all about?"

Moving slowly, Dex circled Wayland's body, leaning in to see more details without stepping too close. Wayland had been shot four times: three in the chest and once in the forehead. Very similar to the way he had found Agnes the night before.

Dropping his gaze to the barn floor, Dex found several shells scattered across the dirt. He could see the prints left by a pair of boots, a man's, slightly smaller than his own. Just like Josh's.

"Dammit," Dex muttered. "Josh, what have you done?"

He stepped outside the barn to draw in deep breaths of fresh air and scanned the horizon. The land stretched away to the pointed, rocky peaks of the mountains surrounding Venom Valley, the color a faded blue as if the sky itself was too tired to try any harder. There was no sign of a rider, no sign of Josh, and Dex cursed on an exhalation.

Why in the hell would Josh shoot Wayland Overbrooke, and then a few days later do the same to Agnes? There was no explanation Dex could think of, and a bubble of doubt about Josh's innocence rose within his chest. He didn't want to believe Josh had shot Agnes and Wayland and then disappeared, but from what he had found, and with Ling Chen's testimony, it seemed his best friend, the man he knew better than anyone, had suddenly become a murderer.

But for what reason?

And what did that say about Dex's own ability to predict a person's reaction? He was a lawman, sworn to enforce the law and protect the people of Belkin's Pass. But if he didn't even know his closest friend was a murderer, the man he thought about at night when he lay alone in his bed, what good was he to anyone else in town?

Dex shook his head and lifted the handkerchief to wipe sweat from his brow. Beating himself up wasn't helping anything or anyone. He needed to stop feeling sorry for himself and get to work.

Pushing aside his self-doubts and frustrations, Dex drew a final breath of fresh air then entered the barn once again and stepped up to crouch alongside Wayland. A cloud of flies lifted away from the body to buzz around his head and he flapped his hands wildly to wave them off. His stomach gurgled a threat as his gaze moved quickly over the corpse, trying not to note how many maggots crawled across the stretched skin and tumbled into the open mouth.

The flies returned in force and drove Dex outside again into the mild warmth of the September sunlight. He tipped his face to the sky and drew in draughts of fresh air. Around him, Wayland's animals bleated and lowed for food. The smell of death from inside the barn had attracted a number of vultures that circled high above, great wings black against the blue sky and white clouds.

As he caught his breath, Dex peered around the small farm. He couldn't just leave it like this. The animals were now part of the estate and under the jurisdiction of the sheriff's office. He was going to have to secure the remaining animals, then pack up Wayland's body and take it back to town for Doc Brandt and the coroner. There was no possibility he'd be able to ride out to the old Stanton house today and look for Josh. Though Dex had a pretty good feeling that was where Josh would run, he knew it would be right at sunset before he even got Wayland's body back to the doc, and he wasn't about to ride that far out of town in the dark of night, no matter how bright of a moon he might have to guide him.

"Damn," Dex muttered and ran the handkerchief over his sweaty brow. He had really hoped to be able to ride out to the old Stanton house and look for Josh. He had a book full of questions to ask him, and he wanted—*needed*—to look into Josh's eyes when he got the answers.

One of the vultures circling overhead let out a cry as if in answer to his plea. Even in the warmth of the sun, a chill skittered up Dex's spine at the sound. He glanced toward the sturdy old farmhouse, the place where Wayland's wife and six children had died of fever not five years prior. Perhaps Josh had gone inside, maybe took some supplies or left a note. Dex hesitated, then decided to get the worst of it over with first. Whatever was in the house would keep.

Tying the handkerchief around the lower part of his face again, like a bandit, Dex took a few last deep breaths of fresh air and stepped back inside the barn to go about settling the animals that remained. He would put off handling Wayland's body until the last, after going through the house.

Once he had tended to the horses, cows, and pigs, Dex took a break to wipe his neck and face with water from Wayland's well. He drank his fill from the cold, clear stream then entered the quiet, stuffy house and looked around. No sign of Josh or anything to explain why Wayland had been shot.

Back outside, Dex tied the wet handkerchief over his nose and mouth once again and stepped inside the barn. Wayland had been a tall man, two or more hands taller than Dex himself. Because of his size, Dex was going to have a tough time getting the body into the back of Wayland's wagon. But, as his mother was fond of saying, there was nothing to be done about it except go ahead and do it.

He lowered the back of the wagon and stepped around to stand above Wayland's head. Holding his breath, he reached down to hook his fingers beneath Wayland's arms and dragged him across the dirt floor. As he quickly stepped backward, Dex noticed Wayland's left foot flopped loosely as it bounced across the uneven dirt. Curious, he lowered Wayland's shoulders and moved around to inspect the man's feet.

The left one was definitely broken, and Dex looked over his shoulder at the broken rung on the hayloft ladder. He stood and looked down at the impression of Wayland's body at the base of the ladder, and at the signs that the straw had been disturbed. It looked as if Wayland had fallen and struggled to stand again. Footprints moved off to circle through the barn. No, not two prints, but rather one footprint and a sliding track alongside it, as if Wayland had walked on his broken ankle. And the dead chickens lay strewn about the sliding track.

A shiver shook Dex's frame even as he stood in the sweltering barn. Whatever had happened, it appeared as though Josh had fired at someone who by all rights should have been dead.

He took a step back from the body and studied it carefully, looking for any sign of life. The corpse lay still as stone, head turned to the side, foot twisted around. Wayland Overbrooke was quite dead, there was no coming back for him now.

As he stared at Wayland's body, Dex noticed the length of his shadow cast by the sun coming in through the open barn doors. He'd spent longer out here than he'd expected and it would be nighttime soon. He needed to get the body back to town, and hopefully before dark. Nothing for it except to get it done.

After several attempts, Dex finally wrangled Wayland's body into the back of the man's wagon and secured the back door. He threw a blanket over Wayland's top half then situated the old, sway-backed mare at the front. With his horse, Nightshade, tied to the back of the wagon, Dex guided Wayland's horse out into the late afternoon sunlight and secured the barn doors. He'd have a couple of men from town ride out tomorrow and bring the rest of the animals to another farm.

Clicking his tongue to the mare, Dex aimed her toward Belkin's Pass and scanned the horizon one last time for any sign of Josh.

"Damn," he muttered and ran his handkerchief over his brow. "Josh, wherever you are, I hope you're safe. Just hunker down and wait for me."

# EIGHT

The sun had passed its zenith and was dropping toward the mountains surrounding Venom Valley by the time Josh guided his horse up the overgrown track to the house where he had once lived. The house sat dark and silent in the weakening light of the sun, the scrub bushes around it casting long shadows as the prairie grass swayed in the wind. Clementine snorted and tossed her head; Josh patted the horse's neck and cooed quietly in her ear until she calmed.

He directed Clementine past the house to the small barn almost overtaken by prairie grass and some kind of vine that looked like small, thin bone in the dying light. The barn was still surprisingly sturdy and Josh dismounted to tug open a door. He led Clem inside and got busy removing the saddle and getting her situated in a small stable where she stood looking at him with wide eyes and twitching ears. In the yard, Josh pumped the old well until his arm muscles burned and, just on the verge of giving up, was finally rewarded with a trickle of cold, clean water. After drinking his fill, he washed the dust and sweat from his face and neck, then stripped off his shirt and splashed water across his chest and beneath his arms.

Josh pushed his arms back into his shirtsleeves as he walked back to the barn where he rooted around until he discovered an old pail. It took several trips back to the pump with the pail until he had filled Clementine's trough. As she dropped her nose into the trough to drink, Josh stepped back outside and tore up armfuls of prairie grass, piling it in a corner of her stall. The horse snuffled fussily at the grass a moment, but finally grabbed several mouthfuls.

With Clementine settled, Josh secured the barn door behind him and returned to the pump to fill the pail again. As the last runner of water splashed into the bucket, he looked the house over. A low, hunched outline against the blood red sky, it appeared to be surprisingly intact for having been vacant so many years.

He knew he needed to get inside and light the stubs of candles before night took the prairie, but his feet seemed stuck. He had no true memories of the place, just hazy images, like dreams before waking. A threatening air seemed to lay around the house, maybe due to the dark windows on either side of the door, so much like Agnes's soulless eyes.

This wasn't the first time he had returned; Dex had ridden out with him twice before. They'd come out once when they'd been young, and Josh had taken a few things from inside the house. The last time they'd come out had been a few years prior, when Dex was still trying to decide if he wanted to become a deputy. He'd remarked that it was a surprise no one had taken over the place, or gone in and broken things. Now, as he stood alone in the dying sunlight, with the weight of shooting Agnes and Wayland heavy on his heart, Josh wasn't sure this had been the best idea for refuge.

Out in Venom Valley, a coyote yipped, startling him out of his thoughts. The mountains that sheltered and contained Venom Valley were nothing more than darker sketches against the darkening sky. He needed to get inside and get settled. There would be no fire tonight; the smoke would only draw any searchers right to him. Tonight he would need to stay cold.

Picking up the pail of water, Josh carried his rifle and the single bag that held all his possessions to the house. The dry hinges shrieked when he pushed open the door and he paused just outside the threshold to stare into the dark interior. A few deep breaths steadied his nerves, and he stepped through the doorway, pausing to turn and look out over the blue-shadowed land stretching away into black. He stood quite still for a time, rifle held tight before him, eyes shifting from shadow to shadow out on the prairie, watching for movement.

Finally satisfied no one had followed him and nothing prowled the land around the house, Josh closed and bolted the door. He located old flints and spent some time striking them over a bowl of dry grass. Darkness and shadow pressed in around him, leaping back with each spark from the flints as his hands shook and he struck the stones faster and more frantically. Chills skittered across his skin and he struggled to keep his focus on the flints, fighting the urge to look around in each flash of sparks in case someone, or something, had been lurking in a dark corner and was closing in on him.

At last, a spark hit the grass just right and it burst into flame, strong and bright in the dark room. Josh tipped an old candle into the quickly fading fire and let out a tense breath when the flame jumped to the wick just as it ate the last of the grass in the earthen bowl. He set the candle in a holder and placed it on the small, rough-hewn table then sat with his back to the wall, eating bread and sipping water as he looked around at the furniture and few belongings.

It was strange to think he had once lived there. It seemed like a story told to him since childhood, the details of which had been so specific he had imagined this place and the objects held within its walls. He had once sat at this very table, slept in that bed. But he could not recall any of it.

After eating some bread and salted meat, he poked through cabinets and drawers, sifting through the items he had already touched during previous trips. There was nothing specific he was looking for; he just hoped something might turn up to explain the reviving dead and the warm, powerful rush of heat he felt around them.

As he sifted through cabinets and storage spaces, Josh felt like an intruder, just like earlier that morning when he'd gone through Wayland Overbrooke's house. Nothing unusual had turned up there either, just the normal items gathered by a man who lived alone. Wayland's house had had a forlorn feeling to it, as though the memories of the man's family haunted every room, every corner, and when Josh had finally left, a heavy sadness weighed on him.

He had avoided the barn; he didn't need the sight of Wayland's corpse to join the memory of the farmer lurching toward him.

The search of his mother's house turned up no new items, and he sat at the table, lost and heartbroken. Had it only been a day since he had shot Agnes? A flash of memory shuddered through him—his first shot punching into her shoulder, the second, her throat, and the final bullet, her forehead, just as she reached for him. Logically, he understood no trace of Agnes had remained inside her stumbling corpse, but the shock and loss sat in his chest like something he couldn't sick up.

Agnes was gone. He would never again be able to talk with her over supper, or be rewarded with her laughter at one of his stories. He would never again step into the house and smell her hearty stew or stand by with a grin as she gave Dex a dressing down about the law's failure to contain the drunken antics of the customers of the One-Eyed Rooster. Never again would he be able to discuss an impressive turn of phrase by a favored author, or debate each side of the civil war, the toll of which could still be seen etched in so many faces, men and women. Once again, his life had changed forever.

The wind picked up, moaning around the house, and a chill shook him. He wished he could light a fire, but the smoke would be a beacon to anyone looking for him. He wondered if Dex was looking for him right now, and, if so, what he was thinking. Surely, Agnes's body had been found by now, and Ling Chen had told what she had seen through the window. What would Dex think, hearing that he had shot Agnes?

Thoughts of Dex made Josh feel even lonelier. Would he ever again be able to talk with Dex, joke with him, ride casually alongside him? Dex was a lawman, through and through, and though Josh shared a close friendship with the man, he didn't think Dex would be able to understand Josh's reasons for shooting Agnes and Wayland. Most likely Josh's claims that the dead had stood up and attacked him would not be seen as a believable defense. He might as well start getting used to the idea of being on his own from here on out.

The grief and loss sitting heavy in his chest ripened into self-pity, and he decided he had done enough thinking for one day. He used an old broomstick to beat the spiders and mice from the thin mattress of the tall, heavy wooden bed set off in the corner. Keeping the rifle by his side, Josh lay down, blew out the candle, and closed his eyes. He shifted position several times, trying to find a comfortable spot on the old mattress, but sleep wouldn't relieve him of his thoughts. He sighed and rolled onto his back, his hand cupping the bulge in his trousers as he thought again about Dex.

He could picture Dex: tall, broad-shouldered, thick, dark hair, and eyes the blue of a clear autumn sky. Beyond his physical traits, however, Dex had a good heart. He was, above all else, a very good man, and Josh had fallen in love with him over the years. He wanted more than anything to lay with Dex, to feel the heat of his body beside him, covering him, feel the prickling brush of Dex's whiskered jaw as they kissed.

He'd heard men talk sometimes as they stumbled drunk out of the Rooster, their words slurred as they rambled about life on the range. About being with men on the range. Josh had a good idea what kinds of things men could and did do with each other, and he'd spun vivid fantasies about himself and Dex.

Josh unbuttoned his trousers and took himself in hand. He closed his eyes and one of the more familiar fantasies played out in his mind. Dex above him, kissing him roughly, his tongue insistent as it filled Josh's mouth. Josh would feel drops of Dex's sweat fall from the man's forehead as Dex thrust the hardened length of his cock into him. Josh wondered what it would feel like to take Dex inside him, to feel him push past the tight ring of muscle and burrow deep inside.

Josh had experimented sometimes, pushing his fingers deep inside himself, pretending it was Dex instead, gasping as his stroke quickened. He could imagine Dex rearing up as he pushed deep into him, his body on the edge of climax. Dex would reach down and take Josh's cock in his big, callused hand and Josh would gasp and buck beneath him. Dex's cock would pin him to the mattress, pumping into him as Dex's hand coaxed the fluttering tingle of orgasm up from Josh's balls. They would come together, Dex releasing his seed deep inside him as Josh's semen spilled onto his chest and belly.

With a deep, lustful grunt, Josh came hard. The first shot landed on his cheek and he gasped at the hot splash of it. When he was spent, Josh lay panting, eyes closed, anxiety melting away in the calming wake of his orgasm. He felt himself slipping into sleep and, though he knew he should clean up first, he stayed on the bed and pulled the old blanket over himself to keep back the chill night air.

Memories disguised as dreams came to him. Flickering images of Agnes as she lurched across the sitting room spun through his mind. He could feel his rifle in his hands but the lever had jammed open. He looked down at the rifle as he backed away and when he looked up again, Agnes stood right in front of him. She reached out and her fingers dug hard into his arms. He struggled to escape but she held tight. Her head pulled back, mouth dropping open wide, wider still, exposing row after row of teeth that glistened in the yellow light of the oil lamp.

Then she dropped her mouth to his neck. Josh screamed as he felt her teeth sink deep into his flesh. He could feel his skin and muscle tear, the hot splash of blood, hear the hungry moan as Agnes tore a raw, slick piece from him.

He awoke screaming, legs kicking, arms flailing. The rifle clattered to the floor beside the bed and Josh sat up, eyes wide, heart pounding. He was covered in sweat and dried semen, dust and dirt clinging to his skin in a greasy paste.

As his breathing slowed, Josh looked around the room, picking out shapes and staring until the items revealed themselves—the chest of drawers; a trunk; the chair where he had draped his shirt.

The terror of his nightmare seeped from his system and he swallowed hard past the dry residue of it lodged in his throat like a clod of dirt. He leaned over the edge of the bed, fingers reaching for the rifle where it lay in a patch of moonlight that spilled in from the window by the bed.

Then a quiet voice spoke from the shadows, "Let me in."

Gooseflesh broke out over Josh's body and he froze, fingertips grazing the wooden stock of the rifle. He swallowed hard and, forcing himself onward, finished his movement and gripped the rifle, bringing it up as he sat upright on the bed.

He scanned the heavy shadows but found no sign of an intruder, so he took a moment to tuck his cock back inside his breeches and use the blanket to wipe himself as clean as possible. Sliding off the bed, Josh crouched in the shadows gathered at the foot. Someone was outside, a man from the sound of it, but one whose voice he did not recognize.

And then the voice came again, floating out of the darkness. It surrounded him, wrapped around him, like a soft, black bed sheet loosed from a drying line. The voice pulled him to his feet and toward the door, soothing and chilling all at once. It called to him in a way that made him want to lay down his rifle and step outside. The words were spoken with an eloquent tongue, touched by an accent that hinted at lands far removed from this flat, dry prairie.

"Open the door," the voice beckoned. "Let me look in your eyes. Let me see your handsome face."

Josh took a step toward the door, then stopped, shaking his head as he gripped the rifle tight. He thought about Dex, conjured the memory of a summer day spent working around Agnes's house. He had been able to smell Dex's work-sweat, could almost smell it again now, that heady scent that made Josh hard in an instant and left his mouth watering.

"I feel you in there," the voice whispered. "Let me in. I won't hurt you."

"No," Josh said through clenched teeth.

"At least open the door," cooed the voice. Josh could hear the pout in his words. "It's so impersonal speaking this way."

Feet moving without thought, Josh drifted through the dark room to the door. He drew back the bolt as if in a dream and pulled open the door.

Moonlight spilled through the doorway to splash across his bare feet and he paused, rifle at his side, hand on the edge of the door. The land stretched away in the cold moonlight. Halfway between the house and the barn, the pump stood at the end of its long shadow. The night was silent, unnaturally so. No insects buzzed, no night birds called. It was as if every living thing had stopped and caught its breath.

But someone, or something, was out there, and it was close. Josh's skin prickled as a wash of cold air curled around him. He shivered and clutched the rifle tight to his chest, his eyes darting around the barren prairie.

"Show yourself," he whispered, lips barely parted.

"As you wish."

A black shape filled the doorway, inches in front of him, appearing out of the air and making Josh's breath catch in his throat. The form blocked out the moonlight and towered over him, standing just outside the threshold. The cold air that had rolled in the door seemed to grow even more frigid, and Josh wondered if he would be able to see his breath.

It was a man, but a man unlike any Josh had ever seen. He was tall, more than six and a half feet, taller even than Dex. In the shadows that cloaked the man's face, Josh could make out a prominent nose and heavy brow. He was clean-shaven and pale, his chin pointed beneath the dark slash of his mouth, and his thick, dark hair hung below his shoulders.

But his eyes were what captured Josh's attention and held him pinned to the spot. In the veil of shadow that concealed the man's face, his eyes gleamed red as embers.

He stared at Josh, into him, and the chill of the air sank into Josh's flesh, biting into his very bones. Inches away, the man turned up a corner of his mouth as his red eyes filled Josh's vision, became his land, his sky, his world, and pushed into the soft meat of his brain.

"Look what we have here," the man said, the sound of his voice soothing Josh's nerves even as the cold rolling off him put Josh on edge. "Where did you stumble in from?"

Josh kept silent, trying in vain to tear his gaze from the man's eyes. But his limbs were locked, frozen by the chill that surrounded him.

The man leaned closer, but remained outside the threshold. He breathed in deep through his nose, closing his eyes. Once those glowing red eyes closed, Josh blinked and shook his head. The fog that had swallowed his brain cleared and he took a deep, freeing breath as the chill within him faded a bit. The man had bewitched him with his gaze.

Josh realized he was in danger, but only if he stepped foot outside the door. He seemed to be safe if he could just keep enough sense to remain inside the house and not invite this stranger in.

"You smell like a rich dessert served with an aged red wine." The man opened his eyes. "And familiar. Or maybe it's just this house. Interesting. What is your name?"

Josh was caught by the man's gaze again and heard himself say, "Joshua."

"Joshua. What a strong name. I am Balthazar. Why don't you invite me inside and we can get to know one another?" He dropped his gaze to the front of Josh's breeches, releasing Josh from his red-eyed hold once again. Balthazar's smile widened, revealing wickedly pointed teeth that gleamed in the moonlight. "I would enjoy seeing more of you."

Josh swallowed past the fear in his throat and forced himself to look away. He licked his lips and, in a voice dry as tumbleweed, managed to say, "No."

Balthazar's voice registered surprise. "You refuse me?"

Josh took a step back, pressed his lips together, and nodded. "I refuse you entrance to this house."

Anger set Balthazar's voice on edge. "You do not invite me inside?"

A tremor started in Josh's stomach and spread out until his whole body shivered. Even without making eye contact with Balthazar he could see the man's red-eyed gaze in his mind. He wanted nothing more than to invite Balthazar inside, let the man have his way with him and take away his grief and uncertainty. But in a corner of his heart, Josh knew once he invited Balthazar inside he would lose his immortal soul, much like Agnes earlier that day. Balthazar was a different breed of evil from what Wayland and Agnes had become, but he was evil all the same.

Josh lifted his gaze as high as Balthazar's torso, avoiding his eyes. "You shall not come inside."

Balthazar pulled back his head and reached out both hands to run his nails down the outer walls to either side of the door. Josh heard the scrape of the man's nails digging into the wood and shuddered.

"If you will not invite me inside, why not step out here? I believe your horse may be in dire trouble." Balthazar flicked the fingers of his left hand and from out on the prairie Josh heard the call of a wolf. Another answered, the howl chilling him to the core. Over the man's shoulder, Josh saw three large shapes lope into view, fur looking silver in the moonlight. The wolves ran straight to the barn to dig and bite at the old wood planks. From inside the barn, Clementine brayed in sudden terror.

Josh reached up to steady himself against the top of the doorframe, struggling to keep from stepping outside and into Balthazar's cold embrace. He could hear Clementine's braying and the snarl and snap of the wolves as they fought to get through the old barn. His stomach rolled and he gripped the top of the doorframe hard in an effort to keep from moving.

His fingers touched on something cold and smooth that lay on top of the doorframe, covered in dust. The chill surface of the object nipped into the skin of his fingers and he ran his hand over it, recognizing it in a sudden flash of memory and grabbing hold of it. He lowered his hand, bringing his find with him, and lashed out, watching as Balthazar's calm demeanor cracked and a glimpse of something dark and hideous briefly revealed itself in the moonlight.

The short silver blade cut deep into Balthazar's arm, releasing a splash of black, vile smelling blood. A brutal cold arced through the blade the moment it touched Balthazar's flesh, biting into the muscle and sinew of Josh's arm and shoulder.

A moment later, in a breeze of movement, Balthazar was gone. He fled into the night, disappearing as silently as he had appeared, leaving Josh standing just inside the threshold of the door and gripping the silver knife that seemed to hum from its contact with him. Josh lingered a moment longer inside the house, sweeping his gaze across the flat, shadowed land stretching away outside the door, but he could tell Balthazar had vanished, taking the cold with him.

Tucking the knife in the pocket of his breeches, Josh stepped outside and raised his rifle to take aim at the wolves digging and biting at the barn. There were three of them, and his first shot struck the largest in the chest. It flopped to the dirt and the two remaining wolves scattered into the night, tails between their legs.

Josh peered into the surrounding night and chambered another round as he crossed the yard to where the wolf whined and pawed at the bloodied dirt, trying to lick the hole in its chest. He shot it in the head and the beast laid still, teeth so similar to Balthazar's as they glittered in the moonlight, and the blood appearing black.

He carried the carcass out into the scrub brush a ways from the house and barn and dumped it by a large stone. Returning to the barn, he opened the door and calmed Clementine, then got her some more prairie grass before striding back to the house, the knife gripped in one hand.

Once safely inside, Josh lit the candle and sat at the table to think. He wasn't sure what Balthazar had been, certainly not human, but he was definitely something different from the revived dead like Wayland and Agnes. This man possessed reason and persuasion. No, something more dangerous than persuasion; witchcraft was more like it. He had almost bewitched Josh into doing his bidding. And he had called the wolves in from the valley to attack the barn.

Now that the danger had passed, exhaustion crept up on him and Josh's eyes grew heavy. He put his head down on the table and surrendered to sleep.

# NINE

Glory did not see the other girls until after sundown, and when they did step out of their dark rooms, they all looked beautiful, even Laura. Their pale skin glowed like the china cups in Sally's cabinet, and their eyes shone with frantic life. Edith rushed up to hug Glory, her lips the color of blood in her pale face, and a feverish glee glittering in her eyes.

"You look more yourself," Glory said as she pulled Edith from around her neck and held the girl at arm's length. Something about the ferocity of Edith's hug made Glory uneasy.

"I feel like a new person," Edith said, and a girlish laugh bubbled from her red lips. "So much better than I did this morning. Do you feel that way, too?"

Glory gave Edith a thin smile. "Seeing you like this makes me feel better."

"Oh, Glory, it's just wonderful." Edith spun in place, her skirt lifting around her legs and earning whistles from a group of men standing by the bar below. Edith laughed and waved to the men, and when she turned back to Glory, a fiery excitement burned in her eyes. Glory reached out for Edith's hand, but the girl had already turned to the steps and was galloping down toward the men waiting below, one hand holding up her skirts to show off her ankles.

Glory leaned on the railing and looked down at the men swarming around the tables and few chairs that had survived the previous night's fight. Whiskey and beer passed over the bar and the girls who had been sick all day threaded their way through the men, trailing fingers over chests and arms and laughing brightly.

"I guess they weren't sick after all."

With a start, Glory looked around to find Sally standing beside her, a glass of clouded green absinthe in one hand. Her hair was done up in a bun with feathers stuck in the back and a velvet green dress flowed down her thin frame. Glory huffed a breath and looked back down at the girls mingling with the men.

"Guess not."

Sally sipped her drink and her eyes glittered like gold nuggets in the light from the lamps. "Going to be a good night." She turned to glare at Glory. "Don't fuck it up again."

Glory watched Sally make her way down the steps and sidle easily into the crowd of men. The woman held herself with a regal air, her back straight and her attention direct as she talked and laughed with the men. A few of the girls led their first customers of the evening up the stairs, giggling as the men reached up beneath their skirts. The couples stepped past Glory without a second look and entered each of the girls's rooms. Doors closed behind them, muffling the excited laughter of the girls and the hungry growls of the men.

With a sigh, Glory made her way down to the first floor. She tried to muster a smile for the men that looked her way, but her heart wasn't in it, and the men seemed to sense it and moved on to the other girls who were decidedly more eager. Glory stood leaning at the end of the bar, watching Clyde pour drinks and collect coins. Something was wrong here in the saloon. It wasn't something you could see just by looking around, but it simmered under the surface. Like a sliver beneath the skin, festering there in secret.

Sometime later, boredom drove Glory back upstairs. Not one man had approached her. Not a surprise considering her mood. She decided to give it up for the night and retire to bed alone. As she climbed the stairs, her steps matched the tune Rusty pounded out on the piano. A man coming down the steps bumped into her, throwing Glory hard into the wall.

"Watch it!" Glory said and, without pausing to think, lashed out, slapping the back of the man's head.

The man stopped with both feet on a step and slowly turned his head to gaze up at her. His eyes were wide and blank, seeming to stare right through her. Beneath the scruff of beard on his neck, Glory could see two marks oozing blood.

"Sorry," Glory said in a quiet voice. "Be more careful."

Blank, almost dead eyes studied her a long moment before the man turned and continued down the steps. Shouldering his way through the drunken men waiting for their special girl to come downstairs again, he stepped out the door into the night. Glory watched the man go, her eyes wide and her heart pounding hard. What had happened to that man?

She had just turned to finish climbing the steps when a

door above opened and another man appeared. He wore the same blank expression as the man who had bumped into Glory, and similar wounds marked his neck. This man held his hat in his hand and clomped down the steps, passing Glory without a look in her direction. Glory watched him pass, her gaze drawn to the bloody wounds in his neck. This man moved through the crowd as the other man had and put on his hat before he vanished out the door into the night.

Glory moved quickly up the steps and flung open the door to Edith's room without knocking. She gasped at the sight before her.

Edith lay on the mattress in her corset, fresh wounds in her neck dribbling blood. The man who Edith had brought upstairs, her third of the night, sat in the straight backed chair, bare-chested, head tipped to the side as another man, broad shouldered and dressed in dark clothes, pressed his lips against the skin of his throat. Two runners of blood ran down over the man's bare chest, the bright red a startling contrast against his pale skin.

"Get away from him!" Glory shouted.

The man lifted his head from Edith's customer's neck and bared sharp, bloodied teeth at her. A shudder of disgust trembled through Glory's stomach followed closely by surprise as she recognized him as the intruder from the night before: Balthazar.

"You!" Glory pointed at him. "You ain't welcome here!"

Balthazar smiled and his tongue slipped out, long and flexible, licking blood from his mouth and chin. Before Glory could react, Balthazar's face was clean and he straightened to his full height, smiling at her. A cold humor sparkled in his red eyes and he rested an elbow on top of the bare-chested man's head as his victim sat and stared straight ahead.

"We meet again, my lovely."

Glory felt the warm pulse of Ohanzee surround her, a gentle reminder that he was near and alert, and it strengthened her courage.

Her hands clenched into fists and she narrowed her eyes. "What kind of devil are you?"

Balthazar laughed and shook his head. "Oh, my half-breed princess, such nerve you have calling me a devil. Look at you, a product of white and Indian coupling, tethered to a Native spirit that, my apologies, dear girl, may as well be a devil himself." He chuckled, a thick, wet sound that came from deep in his throat. "But, I will indulge your curiosity because I have fed well tonight, thanks to your friends, and I'm feeling generous."

His body shivered and suddenly he stood in front of Glory, only inches away. She pulled back, feeling the warm glow of Ohanzee's protection grow stronger, but he did not yet appear in physical form. Balthazar's breath smelled of blood and something dark and dank, reminding Glory of the old well out behind the saloon. His white skin was smooth and unblemished, similar to the other saloon girls. His eyes, blazing red moments before, were now dark, almost black, and stared deep into hers, flicking back and forth, searching.

"Your spirit guide seems to be able to keep you from falling under my control," he said in a low, deep voice. "Very interesting. And, I must admit, frustrating." He leaned away from her. "But, I am being rude. As you know, I am Balthazar, and my home land is far from here."

Glory slowly shook her head, her gaze caught by Balthazar's pointed teeth flashing behind his lips. "California?"

Balthazar threw his head back to laugh and Glory took two

steps back. "You are a dream come true, my dear. After all my years, finally a fresh breath of life." The laugh ended abruptly and he stepped close again, his black eyes boring into hers. "Let's just say I come from a place surrounded by mountains older than you can imagine. My home is leagues upon leagues and eons of agony from this dry, flat land. I was part of a family there, you see, but... Well, let me say that there was a misunderstanding. I was... asked to come here, to your American frontier."

"They drove you off," Glory said, the words touching a memory she tried to keep buried deep.

Balthazar looked at her, his dark eyes seeming to bore straight through her skull and into her brain. "I see you know something of that yourself. Tell me."

She narrowed her eyes and pushed thoughts of her Indian father and white mother from her mind. "I'll not share a thing with you."

Balthazar smiled and leaned in even closer. "One day you'll share that, and so much more with me." He paused to lick his lips, his eyes dropping to stare at her throat. "You see, I am the only one of my kind in your country, the first of what I plan to make a long lineage."

Glory shuddered, turning away from the sight of his sharp teeth and the rank smell of his breath. "And what's that? A demon?"

"No my dear. A vampire."

"Vampire?"

"Yes, vampire." He smiled and held his arms out. "I feed on the blood of the living and will live forever."

Glory glanced around at Edith and the man in the chair, both still and quiet. "You're drinking their blood."

Balthazar smiled. "Very good. You catch on quickly. I

have been feasting up here all night, with the help of your lovely friends."

A ball of hot fury formed in Glory's gut and she narrowed her eyes. "You're a devil and you ain't welcome here."

"Ah, but Edith and your friends have already invited me into their rooms." He bowed, his gaze never moving from her face. "I can come and go as I please."

"You've bewitched Edith," Glory said, her eyes straying to her friend's still, pale form.

"This is not what I call it, but if it's more comfortable for you, it is acceptable to me." Balthazar turned and strode back to the man in the chair, pulling his head to the side to expose his neck. "Now, if you will excuse me, I'm feeling a bit hungry again."

Balthazar opened his mouth wide and Glory caught a glimpse of his teeth, startled to find they looked much longer and sharper than they'd appeared before. He clamped his mouth down on the man's neck with a loud, wet smacking sound that made her jump. She ground her teeth together, hands clenching and releasing as she helplessly watched Balthazar feed.

"Stop it!" Glory shouted. "Leave him be!"

Balthazar ignored her, his mouth pressed against the neck of the man who sat calmly in the chair as if nothing were happening, as if his life wasn't being sucked out of him. As Glory watched, a fresh runner of blood escaped the vampire's lips and rolled down the man's chest.

The sight of the blood snapped Glory from her stunned helplessness and she clasped her hands together over her head. With a wild scream of rage, Glory ran toward Balthazar. She felt the warmth of Ohanzee grow stronger as she ran, and from the corner of her eye she could see the spirit's profile as he raced alongside her. But her focus was Balthazar, specifically the vampire's exposed shoulder, tipped toward her.

When she was just steps from Balthazar, as she was bringing her clasped hands down to strike him, he lifted his head. He opened his mouth, baring his wicked fangs, and the sight of those teeth, his blood-smeared face, and eyes once again blazing red made her gasp. Balthazar seemed to flicker before her, like a candle flame in the wind, and something struck the side of her head. It was a fast, solid blow, faster than Ohanzee could protect her from, and it sent her off her feet. She flew across the room and crashed into the wall. Her head bumped against the rough wood, and something in her neck popped, then everything went black.

# TEN

The feel of fingers on her face, the skin rough, weathered. Glory moaned and turned her head away, tried to lift a hand to push the man off. Confusion and an uneasy sense of distress lingered in her chest. Had she fallen asleep with a man in her room?

Someone patted her cheeks, and now she could hear a voice. It was a woman, her tone impatient, almost angry. Had to be Sally. Maybe Glory *had* fallen asleep with a man in her bed.

"Go 'way," she groaned. Her tongue felt thick and heavy in her mouth. What had happened to her?

"Come on now, dammit, get up."

Glory managed to flutter her eyes open. She squinted at the blurry figure of Sally leaning over her. "Go 'way," she managed again.

Sally straightened, hands on hips, and glared. "She's fine. Now that she's slept off her drink, perhaps she can tell us where Edith's run off to."

Edith. The mention of the girl's name brought everything back in a chilling rush. Glory gasped and sat up fast. Her head spun and a muscle in her neck clenched hard like a fist. She moaned, resting a hand against her forehead. "Oh. What happened?"

"What happened?" a man practically shouted. "Well, Lord, Glory, we were all hoping you could tell us. Nelson Rust is sitting here with his neck gashed open, you're lying on the floor against the wall, and Edith is gone. What the devil happened up here?"

A quick look around the room supported Glory's thinking. Balthazar had left in a rush after knocking Glory across the room, taking Edith with him.

Glory slowly pushed herself up the wall as a cold dread gathered in her gut. Balthazar would turn Edith into a vampire like him, damning the girl's soul for eternity. She could not let that happen to Edith, her only friend in town. Hell, her only friend anywhere.

She steadied herself with her hands against the wall and let her eyes move around the room. The chair where Nelson Rust had been sitting stood across the room, puddles of blood spattered on the floor around the legs. Spots of blood had soaked into the sheets on Edith's narrow bed, and the glass in the window had been busted out, allowing in the dark, chill night air.

With a breath, Glory turned her gaze to the group before her—four burly men and Sally standing in front of them, hands on her hips and her painted mouth curved into a thin frown.

"Well?" Sally demanded. "What the fuck happened up here? I got customers downstairs asking for Edith, and you, for some unknown reason, and other men wanting to know why Nelson Rust was carried out with bloody rags held to his neck." She stepped forward, one bony finger extended to point at Glory's nose. "Start talking, you half-breed bitch. And I better like what I hear, or you'll swing like your father."

Anger burned into life in Glory's chest, sending heat flaming up into her face. Her fingers curled into fists and she narrowed her hardened gaze on Sally's face. The saloon owner lowered her hand and took a step back, looking surprised and uneasy. The men behind Sally shifted their weight and looked away. A couple men rubbed their hands on the backs of their necks in discomfort.

Glory tried to keep her voice even as she spoke. "I came up here to check on Edith. There was a man in here with her."

"Nelson Rust," Sally said.

"No," Glory said, then closed her eyes and shook her head, wincing at the pain in her neck. "Yes. Nelson was here, too. But another man was with them."

"Edith does two at once?" one of the men whispered to the man beside him, then pressed his lips closed tight when Sally snapped her head around to glare at him.

"Who else was up here?" a big, beefy bear of a man asked. Glory thought his name was Bob Cockburn, but couldn't be sure. He preferred the girls with blonde hair and didn't spend much time talking to her.

"A man I've seen in the saloon before." Glory shifted her gaze back to Sally. "He was in here after hours. He's... he's a dangerous man. I came up here to check on Edith and found him here. He's from a country far away. His name is Balthazar and he was... cutting Nelson Rust around the neck. When I tried to stop him he knocked me across the room. If he's gone, he must have taken Edith with him."

"Well for fuck's sake," Sally grumbled. She hung her head a moment, then turned to look at the men behind her. "All right, get outside and start looking for a trail. The man who brings Edith back gets the girl of his choice for free for a week."

The men's eyes brightened and they fled the room as a group, leaving Sally and Glory alone. Chill air blew over Glory through the broken window, making her nipples harden and gooseflesh crawl across her arms. She kept her palms flat against the wall behind her as she stared at Sally. The woman took a step toward her, saw the expression on her face, and retreated again.

"I don't know what's going on here," Sally said in a quiet voice. "But as sure as I know the sun will rise in the East tomorrow morning, I know you're involved somehow."

Glory stepped toward her and Sally backed off two steps, her expression shifting to fear. Keeping her feet planted where she stood, Glory leaned in. She said in a quiet voice, "The saloon isn't safe. You should leave."

Sally's eyes widened, and then she threw back her head and laughed. It was a brittle, bitter cackle, and Glory could hear just how close to the edge of sanity the years of absinthe had pushed the woman. The laugh softened to a gurgle in Sally's throat and she lowered her chin to stare at Glory, eyes glazed as if she suffered from fever.

"What do you know of being safe?" Sally snarled. "You've been on the run your entire life, never putting down roots, keeping everyone at arm's length. You'll be dead inside of six years and leave nothing behind to show you ever walked the dirt of this land."

"You'll see," Glory said, keeping her anger in check as best she could. "He's gotten to all the girls here already, except you, me, and Beatrice. Plus he's gotten to who knows how many in town by now. He'll not take you because you've poisoned your blood with drink."

The slap came fast and rocked Glory's head back. Her cheek burned and, too late, she could feel the warm glow of Ohanzee pulse around her. If only she could talk with her spirit protector, she'd like to ask him why he saved her from some things, but couldn't manage to keep her from others.

Glory lifted a hand to her throbbing cheek. Beneath the broken window she could hear the group of men talking to one another, searching for a trail to track down Edith and the girl's captor.

"I've warned you," Glory said, and brushed past Sally to leave Edith's room. She walked down to her room and began to gather her things.

"If you leave here tonight, don't expect to ever come back," Sally said from the doorway.

"If I leave here tonight, someday you'll beg me to come back." Glory turned to look at the woman over her shoulder. "And I'll turn you down."

One of the girls, Hazel, drifted past behind Sally, walking backward as she pulled along a man by the hand. From the bulge in the man's breeches, Hazel had been whispering in his ear for quite some time down in the saloon. The man was staring into Hazel's face with a dazed expression and Glory's stomach trembled in fear. Balthazar had turned some of the girls into vampires like him, and now they were turning the men they brought to their rooms. Soon everyone in town would be a vampire like him.

Glory shifted her gaze back to Sally's narrow, sunken face. "Hear me well, Sally. This town is no longer safe. Heed my warning and leave while you can. There's evil here you can't understand."

Sally turned her head, no doubt watching Hazel lure the bewitched man into her room. The door down the hall clicked shut and Sally turned back to Glory.

"Nothing happening here but what happens every other night. Men enjoying themselves with my girls." She turned and drifted out of sight, leaving the doorway empty and Glory's heart in her throat. She resumed packing her things and couldn't decide how she felt when she finished sooner than expected. Sally's words seemed to echo in her head: *You've been on the run your entire life, never putting down roots, keeping everyone at arm's length. You'll be dead inside of six years and leave nothing behind to show you ever walked the dirt of this land.*

Glory closed her eyes and forced Sally's words from her mind. She had to focus on finding Edith. Maybe there was some way to change her back, she didn't know, but she had to try. Edith was the only friend she had ever had, and she would not let her be taken away without a fight.

She pulled on her coat, a thin, forest green garment she had found discarded in a previous town. She lifted her bag, spared a moment for one last glance around the small, cramped room. She had spent so many hours in this room, entertaining any number of men, all the while thinking of Ohanzee, her spirit protector and love. The voices and laughter of the men in the saloon below were growing louder as they drank more, and soon those looking for a fuck would start asking for any available girl. Glory shuddered and, lifting her chin, stepped from her room and turned toward the stairs. After walking several feet, she came to an abrupt stop.

Three of the other girls of the saloon stood in a line across the narrow second floor balcony, blocking her way to the stairs. They all stared at her, eyes glittering in the gaslight of the lamps.

"Where you off to, Glory?" Anne asked. She ran her tongue over her lips.

"Step aside," Glory said, trying to keep her voice even. She adjusted her grip on the handle of her worn carpetbag and shifted her gaze from one girl to the other as the warm glow of Ohanzee surrounded her. Her voice still shook, however, because she was starting to learn there were some things Ohanzee had no power to protect her from. "I'm taking my leave of this place."

"But, Glory," Laura moaned. "We don't want you to go. We could have such fun together." She parted her lips and Glory shivered at the sight of Laura's pointed teeth.

"I know what you all are," Glory stammered. "I won't let you make me into one of you."

All three girls took a step toward her and Glory backed away. She had moved past the door to Laura's room now and was backing along the second floor balcony. Her room was the third door behind her, but that would provide little protection. She needed to get off the balcony or else she'd be trapped; the girls were herding her toward the wall just beyond Hazel's door.

"Oh, but Glory, it feels so good," Carmen said. "You can't begin to imagine the power."

With one more step back, Glory decided on a course of action. She made a quick move toward the balcony as if she were going to throw herself over the railing. The three girls flew toward the railing, moving faster than Glory could track. Seconds later, the three realized she had duped them and swung around, hissing. Carmen crouched on the narrow balcony railing, mouth open wide to display her pointed teeth, and Glory turned away to fumble at Beatrice's door. Her sweaty palms slipped around the smooth knob, unable to find a purchase.

She could feel the strengthening pulse of Ohanzee's spirit around her and knew the girls were approaching, moving slowly, toying with her like a barn cat tortures a mouse. The doorknob finally caught and she pushed into the room, turning to slam the door shut.

"What the fuck you doing?" a man shouted from the bed in the corner of the room.

Glory didn't even glance in that direction. She grabbed a straight-backed chair and wedged it beneath the knob, then picked up her bag and turned toward the window.

"Glory!" Beatrice cried, "What the blazes are you on about?"

Glory turned her head to look at Beatrice where the girl sat astride her man's hips. Both were nude, Beatrice's full breasts hanging low, nipples large and dark in the low lamplight. Glory looked away, moving fast to the window. It was like the window in her room, secured in the middle of the frame with a rod that allowed it to pivot, the top coming into the room and the bottom pushing out. She opened the lock and pushed the bottom out, dropping her bag to the ground.

A hand gripped her shoulder and Glory shrugged it off, turning with her fist up and her jaw set. Beatrice stood behind her, anger leaving the girl's face at the sight of Glory's expression.

"You're terrified," Beatrice said. "What's got you in such a state?"

The girls outside pounded and the door rattled in its

frame. Glory nodded toward the door, glimpsing the man on the bed sit up and fish for his clothes on the floor, nervous eyes fixed on the door.

"Don't give them permission to enter your room," Glory said as she turned back to the window and slipped one leg over the sill. "They're vampires."

"They're what?" Beatrice said, frowning at her in confusion.

"Demons that drink the blood of the living," Glory explained. She straddled the windowsill as the girls pounded on the door and it trembled. Suddenly, the pounding stopped and the room went quiet. Glory thought she knew what that meant, and she moved quickly.

She clutched the edge of the sill, swung her other leg out the window and let herself hang a moment before letting go. She dropped several feet to the hard packed dirt behind the saloon and fell on her ass, teeth clicking together and the thump of her landing rattling up her spine.

"Glory!"

She looked up at Beatrice's pale face sticking out of the window above her. "Where you going?"

"Far away from town." Glory got to her feet and had just reached down to pick up her bag when Ohanzee's protective glow burst around her. Strong though it was, it wasn't enough to keep one of the girls from grabbing her.

She felt the wet heat of the girl's mouth near her neck and instinctively brought her shoulder up, knocking her attacker in the jaw. Glory spun out of the girl's grip and turned to find Carmen crouched low like a mountain lion, the girl's red, gleaming eyes fixed on her throat.

CHAPTER

# ELEVEN

Dex stepped down from Wayland Overbrooke's wagon as the long shadows of sunset were coming together to make full-on night. Wayland's horse snorted and stamped uneasily at the smell of her owner's decaying body on the chill evening breeze.

"Easy, girl." Dex made his way to the back of the wagon to untie his own horse and secured the reins to the hitching post outside Doc Brandt's office. A light glowed in a back window of the long, narrow building. It was the examining room farthest from the street, the one Doc used for bodies.

Dex climbed the two steps to the raised boardwalk and turned to look out along the street. The night was laying claim to the town, stripping the sunlight from the sides of the buildings and faces of folks hurrying toward home. Down a ways, across from the sheriff's office, the doors to the One-Eyed Rooster stood open, the sounds of the piano and hard laughter of men on their way to drunk rolling out into the night. The high-pitched laugh of one of the saloon girls floated down to him, almost musical in its lilting rhythm.

The door behind him opened, causing Dex to jump and snap his head around. Doc Brandt stood in the doorway with his coat on and hat in his hand, eyes wide with surprise.

"Deputy," Doc Brandt said, his voice scratchy and tired. "You'll have my full report on Agnes Pritchett in the morning, when I update the Sheriff."

Dex let out his breath. "Well, Doc, much as I wish that's why I was here, I got some bad news for you."

Doc Brandt narrowed his eyes a moment, then looked down at the body wrapped in sheets in the back of the wagon. He pursed his lips as he took in the sight.

"That Wayland Overbrooke's wagon?"

"Yep."

Doc turned his gray eyes back to Dex. "And I suppose that's Wayland himself beneath that blanket?"

Dex nodded and leaned back on the railing. "Yep."

Doc left the door open and moved to the edge of the stairs. He ran the brim of his hat around and around in his fingers, his shoulders slightly slumped with fatigue.

"Was he shot?"

"Yep." Dex moved up beside Doc. "Four gunshot wounds, including one in the forehead."

Doc turned his head fast, then winced at a pain in his neck. "Like Agnes?"

"Just like Agnes." Dex leaned in closer to Doc. "Looked like he fell off the ladder to his hayloft and broke his ankle. Laid in the straw for a while, maybe days, then got up and helped himself to his chickens."

Doc's nose wrinkled in distaste. "He ate his chickens?"

"Feathers and all." Dex took a breath. "Then someone shot him four times. Three in the chest and once in the forehead."

"Almost exactly like Agnes," Doc muttered and looked down at the covered body glowing in the pale blue moonlight. A thought struck him and he turned again to squint at Dex. "Have you found Josh Stanton yet?"

Dex looked away, his gaze snagged by the warm light thrown through the doors of the One-Eyed Rooster. His throat craved the burn of whiskey and his brain begged for some relief from the thoughts spinning through it, relief only whiskey could bring.

"No. Not yet," he finally replied, turning back to him. "I don't want to think Josh is involved in this. I can't imagine he would just up and start shooting people, especially not Agnes. I need to find him and talk to him."

"Well, you're going to have to get to him before the Sheriff does." Doc's voice sounded tired all of a sudden, drained. "Once he finds out about Agnes, he'll want to find Josh. You know he respected that woman almost as much as his own mother."

Dex nodded. "I know."

"My guess is he'll get a party together tomorrow and go out looking for Josh," Doc said. "But you probably know that."

"Yep, I do. I just need to find him first." Dex lifted his chin toward the wagon. "Want me to take Wayland inside for now?"

Doc blew out a breath and pulled a pocket watch from his vest, angling his body to see the time in the light from his office.

"The missus is already mad, I'm certain. Take the wagon around back and I'll open the door. I've finished my examination of Agnes. We can move her to the outer shed for Samuel."

Dex nodded and thought Samuel Hardy, the undertaker,

hadn't had this much business in one week since the four Creighton boys had tried to rob the bank and ended up being shot by the customers and the bank owner. He climbed into the wagon and directed the mare around the back of Doc's office where the man stood in silhouette looking out. They wrapped Agnes in an old bed sheet and carried her stiff body to a small shed out back that Doc used for overflow, then maneuvered Wayland's longer, heavier form up the steps and down the short hall to take her place.

"May as well give the missus the chance to really light into me and take a quick look." With a sigh, Doc removed his coat and nodded toward the oil lamp across the room that Dex crossed to light. They peeled back the sheet and Doc leaned in close to examine Wayland's face, not even flinching as he said, "Quite a few maggots here, Deputy."

"I tried to get as many of them off as I could," Dex said, not sure if he wanted to be impressed or frightened at Doc's lack of revulsion at Wayland's condition. Just what kind of steel had been fitted inside Doc's spine? He had heard once that Doc had worked as a surgeon on the battlefields during the Civil War, but the man never spoke of his past.

"Grab a forceps and pick them off while I look him over," Doc grumbled, seating his glasses on the end of his nose.

Dex steadied his stomach and set about plucking maggots and other insects off Wayland's skin and out of the folds of his clothes, dropping them in a steel basin. He tried to convince himself the body before him was not the corpse of a man he had known all his life, but an old rotted log and that he was simply collecting bait to fish in the stream, but it was tough. As he lifted the squirming white maggots, Doc spread open Wayland's dirty shirt and held the oil lamp close as he peered at the bullet wounds.

"No blood," Doc muttered. Gray eyes looked at Dex over the tops of glasses. "Four shots. Three to the chest and one to the forehead. All with no blood."

"Does that mean something?" Dex asked.

"Means his heart wasn't beating when he was shot," Doc said and straightened up, turning away to set the lamp back down.

"Then he was already dead when he was shot?"

Doc turned his head to snap over his shoulder, "Well if his heart wasn't beating, he sure as hell wasn't alive."

Dex bit back an angry response. "What about Agnes?"

Doc turned to glare at him. "What about Agnes?"

"Was there blood around her wounds?"

Doc blew out a frustrated breath and stomped across the room to the water basin where he dipped in his hands. "Suppose there wasn't, what would you say?"

"That she was already dead when she had been shot, too."

"And that would be nice, wouldn't it?" Doc muttered. "Get your friend Josh off the hook because there ain't no law against shooting a corpse." Doc dried his hands on a towel then removed his glasses and wiped the lenses with his shirttail.

"Someone is using corpses for target practice." Dex turned back to the body and harvested the last maggot in sight, then set the basin aside and covered it with a towel.

"Corpses that are upright at the time they're shot," Doc said. "Or else the shooter stands directly over them."

Dex rinsed his hands in a bowl of water, dried them with a fresh towel and turned to look across the body at Doc. "Did you find anything else on Agnes?"

Doc put on his glasses and worried his hands. He seemed

agitated to Dex, as if he was trying to understand the strange things he had found on these two bodies. "You asked me to look at her fingers. There were splinters beneath the nails of her left hand." Doc slipped a glance his way. "No blood around those, either."

"So she was dead when she did it."

Doc glared at him. "Damnation, Deputy! You're just trying to get me to say these folks have stood back up and started walking again after dying, aren't you?"

"Doc, what other explanation is there?"

"I'm not right sure off the top of my head." He snapped the sheet back over Wayland's corpse, put his hands on his hips and narrowed his eyes at Dex. "I will admit to being balled up about these two bodies, but I'm not going to the Sheriff and tell him some bosh about the dead gettin' up and walkin' around. Next thing you know I'll be sent packing."

Dex paused to take a breath and, clenching his jaw, looked at the scuffed and dirty toes of his boots. Doc Brandt was frustrated, he knew that, but the man was seeing everything Dex had seen himself. Why couldn't he come to the same conclusions as Dex?

Doc walked up and put a hand on his shoulder. It was cold from being in the chill water of the basin. The feel of it made Dex think back on lifting Wayland into the back of the wagon. Dex managed to suppress a shudder and lifted his gaze to look in Doc's face.

"Now, here's what I suggest," Doc said, his voice softer, gentler, after his blow up. "Go down to the Rooster. Have some drinks, hell, have a girl. Put all this stuff about corpses walking around and Josh Stanton out of your mind. Get some sleep and tomorrow morning, everything will look clearer."

Dex held Doc's gaze a long moment, then pressed his lips tight and gave a quick nod. "All right. I know I've kept you from your supper long enough." He turned to pick his hat from the peg on the wall, pulling his shoulder out from under Doc's cold hand with the movement. "Give my regards to your missus."

Doc extinguished the oil lamp and followed Dex out of the room, carrying the insect-filled basin. Leaning out the back door, Doc tapped the basin against the steps, spilling the bugs on the dirt. He closed and locked the door, left the basin on a table, and followed Dex out the front where he locked that door as well. Turning to face Dex, Doc put on his hat then, nodding to him once, pulled out his pocket watch and hurried off down the road, muttering about his supper.

A step toward the stairs down to the road allowed Dex to look up and see the quarter moon hanging overhead, the bone-white points sharp enough to cut night sky. The wind, colder now, made his thoughts turn to Josh and he hoped he'd found someplace warm to ride out the night.

After setting up Wayland's horse in the small stable behind the doctor's office, Dex decided to take Doc Brandt's advice and led Nightshade down the street to tie him up outside the One-Eyed Rooster. He stood for a moment in the wash of yellow gaslight and white moonlight, then climbed the steps and walked in the door.

Conversation lagged briefly when Dex walked in, as he expected it would. Tight expressions from all the men, some of whom looked guilty of something as well. But Dex wasn't there as a lawman; he had come as a man looking to forget.

He shouldered his way through the men standing three deep at the bar until he reached the far end. A very drunk, very dirty, and grizzled man staggered off a stool at the sight of his approach and Dex slid onto it. He nodded to the bartender, Clyde, when the man held up a whiskey bottle and, when the glass was set before him, swallowed it down. The liquor burned his throat and caught his breath in its fiery fist, finally settling in his gut like a sun-warmed river rock.

"Deputy," a woman purred beside him. "Have you come here to arrest me?"

Dex slid his eyes to the side and hoped his impatience did not show in his expression. He did not feel up to social niceties; he just wanted to be left alone and have a few drinks. "Evenin' Sally." He looked around at the men who had all returned to their conversations and flirtations with the girls. "Business looks good."

Sally swirled the contents of her drink, hidden inside a silver goblet, as she looked around the room as well. Dex would bet all he owned it was absinthe.

"I can't complain." She turned back to him. "So, are you here for business or pleasure?"

Dex caught Clyde's eye and lifted his empty glass for a refill, then looked back at Sally. "I've come to remember how to forget."

She smiled and raised her glass to him. "You've come to the right place." Sally lifted her chin to Clyde. "The Deputy drinks for free tonight."

"You don't have to do that," Dex said as Clyde nodded and set the bottle by Dex's right hand.

Sally touched his shoulder and leaned down to whisper in his ear. "Drinks are free, Deputy. Anything else is going to cost you." She smiled and drifted off into the crowd.

Dex sipped the second glass of whiskey and kept his

head down, staring at the scarred and polished surface of the bar. Thoughts of Agnes and Wayland spun through his mind, tangling with memories of Josh and snippets of conversation he'd had with Doc Brandt. Somewhere in all of it there had to be some explanation, a reason for it all to be happening.

A sound drew his attention from his thoughts and he raised his gaze to the room. Several of the men were looking up at something on the second floor. Dex looked up as well and was surprised to see one of the saloon girls perched on the railing. She had her back to the room below, knees bent, and a hand between her feet holding herself steady. She looked like a large bird, dressed in bright colors with a wave of dark hair flowing down her back. He heard the girl hiss before she jumped from the railing to the second floor balcony and out of sight.

Frantic pounding on one of the upstairs doors followed and Dex turned back to his whiskey. Clyde gave him an uneasy look and, with a sigh, Dex downed the last of his third drink. He pushed the bottle back at the bartender and got to his feet just as the pounding upstairs stopped. Standing at the bar, he watched three of the girls run down the steps, their feet seeming to barely touch the wood risers. The trio flew through the saloon without sparing the group of men, their bread and butter, a second glance. As they rushed past, Dex caught a glimpse of red eyes and white, pointed teeth before they disappeared down the back hallway and out the rear door toward the privy.

"Too much beer, I guess," one man in the crowd cracked, and the others let out roars of laughter.

A small, cold ball of unease had formed in Dex's gut,

however, and he did not laugh. Those red eyes and pointed teeth stayed in his memory like a photograph. He pulled his Colt from the holster and eased down the back hallway after the girls.

# TWELVE

"**B**ehind you!"

The warning came from Beatrice above her, and it most likely saved Glory's life. She dodged aside, just in time to avoid Laura who had rushed her from behind, and the girl flew past Glory to crash into Carmen. The two girls rolled across the dirt, giving Glory the opportunity to turn to run. But she found Anne standing before her. Beyond Anne, Glory noticed the pile of wood that she and Edith had made last night from the saloon's broken tables and chairs. She needed a weapon if she were going to fight off three of them at once, and several of those pieces of wood had sharp, jagged ends.

Glory bent her knees slightly, her eyes on Anne and her ears alert for any sounds from Carmen and Laura behind her. Moving slowly, Glory lowered herself to grab a handful of dirt. With a burst of strength, she rushed Anne and threw it in the girl's face. Anne hissed and turned her face away, giving Glory an opening to dart past and grab a table leg from the pile of wood. She held the narrow end and jabbed the ragged, splintered part at Anne.

"Why are you fighting us so hard, Glory?" Anne snarled. "You have been held down your whole life because you're a half-breed. Think of how good it would feel to avenge those comments."

"You're a demon," Glory said. "And I'll have no part of demons."

Glory caught a flash of movement from the corner of her eye and suddenly felt herself falling to the side. The warm shell of Ohanzee's protection burned around her, hotter than her room upstairs in the still, sun-drenched days of August. She brought her arms up, holding tight to the splintered table leg and bracing the flat end against the hard packed ground by her side.

Carmen leaped at her, the space she covered impossible, practically flying through the still night air. Glory heard Beatrice and the man she had been fucking give shouts of surprise in the window above, and then the table leg stabbed into Carmen's chest.

Glory looked up into Carmen's anguished face, saw the points of her sharp teeth as her mouth stretched wide to release an unearthly scream that filled Glory's chest with icy dread and sent shivers up her spine. And then a flood of dark, black blood poured from the girl's mouth. Glory pressed her lips together and closed her eyes, turning her face and her shoulders to avoid the worst of it.

Tipping the table leg away, Glory let Carmen's body topple to the ground and scrambled to her feet, her shoes slipping in the thick, dark blood around her. With wide eyes locked on Carmen's body, Glory backed away from it.

"Murderer!" Laura shouted as she rushed toward Glory.

The girl's eyes glowed red in the dark, and Glory turned toward the pile of wood, but she was too slow. Laura grabbed her with strong fingers, her nails like claws that tore the fabric of her green coat now soaked with Carmen's blood. The saturated material of the coat peeled away in Laura's hands, and Glory pulled her arms free to stagger toward the pile of wood. She grabbed a chair leg and spun around. Laura threw the tattered and blood soaked coat to the ground as Anne suddenly appeared beside her, both of their eyes glowing like embers in the night.

"Here now!" a male voice called. "What's going on out here?"

Glory turned to look. The deputy—Dex, that was his name—had stepped out the back door of the saloon, his gun drawn and jaw set. Behind him, two drunk men stepped outside as well, still clutching glasses of beer.

"Go back inside!" she shouted, but it was too late. Anne and Laura jumped toward the men, pressing their faces into the exposed throats of the two drunks. The men screamed and Glory caught a glimpse of bright red gushers of blood soaking their shirts before she turned away.

She heard the sound of gunfire and kept her head down as she crossed to pick up her bag. With the table leg still in hand, she fled around the side of the saloon.

Several horses stood out front, tied to the rails of the saloon's porch and skittish from the smell of blood in the air. Glory dropped the chair leg and untied the nearest horse, then climbed in the saddle and kicked the animal into motion, heading out of town and toward the only people who might even consider taking her in and providing her with protection.

# THIRTEEN

Dex could not seem to keep track of the girls out behind the saloon. They moved fast, faster than any one, man or woman, should be able to. Right after he'd shouted, the girls seemed to flicker in the moonlight, like candle flames, then suddenly pounced on the men beside him, driving them to the ground.

"Get off them!" Dex shouted and fired a few shots in the air to try and frighten the girls away, but to no avail.

He glanced over, watching as the half-breed girl grabbed her bag and disappeared around the side of the saloon. Every instinct told him to go after her, to find out what she knew about these girls and how they could move so fast, and he took a few steps in her direction before the screams of the men being attacked fell silent. Blood pooled on the ground beneath them and the girls seemed to be drinking it from the wounds on the men's throats.

"Leave them!" Dex fired more shots in the air.

One of the girls turned to him, bloody mouth open wide to reveal wicked, sharp teeth. She hissed and, in another disquieting flicker of movement, suddenly stood in front of him.

Dex took two steps back and started to raise his gun. The girl put a hand to his chest and gave a push that sent him sprawling. He landed on his back, his head tapping against the hard dirt and leaving him dizzy. The girl straddled him, her thighs clutching either side of his chest, squeezing his ribs hard and making it impossible for him to breathe. He opened his mouth and tried to catch a breath, but she wouldn't let him.

She leaned down, bloody mouth drawn up in a smile, and tore open his shirt. Then she shrieked as if he had branded her and suddenly the pressure on his sides eased. Dex rolled to one side, drawing in deep, grateful breaths.

After a few moments, he scrambled backward, shirt hanging open to expose the white of his undershirt beneath. His gold cross bounced against the soft material and glowed in the moonlight. His father used to wear it, and then his mother had given it to him after his father disappeared. Had that scared the girl off?

He got to his feet, his sides sore where the girl had held him, and picked up his gun from the ground. The two men lay dead, throats torn open, staring eyes filled with moonlight. The girls were nowhere to be seen.

Dex looked across at the body of the girl Glory had stuck with the table leg and, as he watched, it trembled in the gentle wind and collapsed in on itself. He crossed the dirt, avoiding the puddles of thick, black blood, and crouched by the body. It looked as though someone had set her on fire and she had turned into ash.

He looked up at the moon, then over at the door where two more men appeared. The men saw the bodies and their eyes widened before they turned to rush back inside the saloon.

Dex stood and holstered his weapon as he made his way back to the door. He needed to keep the other men inside, and then let Wallace, the other deputy, know what had happened. The sheriff would be returning tomorrow, and once he learned about Agnes and Wayland, he'd most likely form a posse to hunt Josh down.

If Dex wanted to save Josh, he was going to have to ride out to the house on the edge of Venom Valley and look for him, no matter what time of night.

# FOURTEEN

Josh sat up straight in the chair and let out a gasp. He fumbled the silver knife and it fell to the wood floor, the point sticking in the plank and the sound making him jump. Leaning down, he pulled the knife free and held it in both hands, arms outstretched, eyes wide as he looked frantically around the dark house, trying to find substance in the shadows.

He was alone.

A shaky breath slipped from between his lips, but his relief was short lived as he remembered the stranger, Balthazar, who had called the wolves. He shot out of the chair, knocking it over backward in his haste, and peered out the dirty window at the dark world outside. The moon had gone down, but the stars were bright enough to reveal that the barn still stood intact, the doors secure. There was no sign of wolves.

He must have had a bad dream, but for the life of him he couldn't recall any of the details. Maybe that was for the best, though. He cast another look through the window at the property he could not remember living on, then turned in time to see the door ease open. His heart staggered in his chest and he looked at the rifle he had left behind on the table, the weak candlelight glinting off the dark metal of the barrel. All he had to protect himself was the small silver knife.

A tall, broad shouldered figure slipped through the doorway and Josh tightened his grip on the knife. He pressed his lips together as his heart raced in his chest and the intruder took two more cautious steps inside the house, clearing the door.

Josh stepped forward, trying to be silent, but the creak of a board beneath his foot gave him away and the intruder moved away, leaving the blade to slice through the sleeve of his coat. The man turned, bringing up a gun as Josh crossed to the table and snatched up his rifle, chambering a round as he spun. They stood looking at one another a moment, both men panting, until Josh finally swallowed and said, "Dex?"

Dex lowered his pistol and straightened up, his hat brushing the low ceiling. He ducked and reached up to take the hat from his head, the dim candlelight flickering in his dark hair. Turning his arm, he inspected the split in his sleeve before narrowing his eyes at Josh.

"Nice way to greet a friend."

Josh lowered the rifle. "Sorry. It's been... It's been a strange few days."

"Yeah, lot of that goin' around." Dex pushed the door shut. He shrugged out of his coat and looked over the cut in the sleeve again, then grumbled something that sounded to Josh like, "This was a good coat."

Dex righted the chair where Josh had fallen asleep, but he didn't sit down.

They looked at each other a moment, then Dex said, "Want to tell me what's going on?"

Josh placed the rifle on the table, looking away from Dex's gaze. He had no idea what Dex knew. Maybe he hadn't talked to Ling Chen. Maybe no one had found Agnes's body yet. And probably no one knew that Wayland Overbrooke was dead. He would need to speak carefully and not give too much away. Dex was his friend, but he was also a deputy.

"Not sure what you mean," Josh said. "Just came out to the old house for a night, that's all."

Dex rounded the table and stepped up close to him. Josh felt the heat of Dex's body surround him, soak into him. The salty-sweet smell of Dex's sweat made his pulse jump as Josh looked up into Dex's blue eyes, made pale by the candlelight. They stood staring at each other a long, silent moment, the room dark around them, Dex's intentions a mystery.

Until Dex finally said, "I found Agnes."

Josh fought to keep his expression neutral. "Where was she?"

"Dammit, Josh!" Dex stomped across the room, throwing his hands in the air before spinning to point an accusatory finger at him. "Stop fucking playing with me and just talk to me." He paused to take a few breaths, trying to calm himself. Regret gnawed into Josh's gut as he realized it was the first time Dex had had to calm himself down when talking with him. Everything in his life had changed.

"Ling Chen rode into town last night," Dex continued, his voice quiet, tired. "She was scared out of her wits because she saw you shoot Agnes." Dex crossed to stand before him again, the muscles in his jaw tight, anger and doubt rolling off him. "Why would she say that?"

"You here to arrest me?" Josh moved to put the table between them and gave Dex a cool look. This entire scene felt so wrong. Dex was his best... Hell, his *only*, friend. Josh should be able to trust him with everything he thought or felt. But Dex was also a lawman, and Josh had, in fact, shot both Agnes and Wayland, several times.

The fact that they had already been dead would be difficult to explain, and most likely wouldn't matter.

Dex sighed and dropped his gaze. He looked around the dark room and rubbed his hands together. "It's freezing in here. Do you have any firewood?"

Josh shook his head. "I didn't want to light a fire."

"Well, now that I've found you, how about we warm up?" Dex strode outside and Josh moved to stand in the doorway, watching him root around in the prairie grass and scrub bush for sticks and branches. A few minutes later, Dex returned with his arms full and Josh bolted the door behind him.

He sat at the table, hands clenched tight before him as he watched Dex build the fire. The material of Dex's shirt stretched tight over his muscles, and Josh noticed that the back of his dark hair had grown past his collar. He hadn't seen Dex in over a week. Josh's chores and Dex's increased hours to cover for Sheriff Haden had kept them both occupied. And though this had been the worst week of Josh's life, and he had no idea of Dex's true intentions, he was glad to see him.

A chilled sadness rose in him, though, when he realized this might be the last time they would spend together. This conversation would most likely change their relationship. Either Josh would open up and tell Dex everything, or he would lie, pit his word against Ling's and see which the town would believe.

The flints looked small in Dex's hands, and after a few sure strikes, flames roared in the fireplace. Warm air filled the room and something within Josh's chest that had been clenched since earlier that week, perhaps longer, eased just a bit. Maybe he could get Dex to understand.

Brushing bits of wood and soot from his hands, Dex sat opposite Josh at the table. He clasped his rough fingers together and leaned down to lock his eyes with Josh's. They sat that way for a long time while the fire popped and crackled beside them.

Finally, Josh blinked and looked away, reluctantly tearing his gaze from Dex's blue eyes. "I didn't shoot Agnes." His stomach trembled as he stood on the edge of explaining what he'd seen that week, of saying aloud his suspicions.

Dex sat back and spread his hands. "No? Then who did? And why did you run?"

Josh took a breath and thought a moment. He needed to go back further to explain it, and he really needed to tell Dex everything. He owed the man that much, at least, before Dex arrested him.

"Do you remember Old Man Ogden's funeral?" Josh asked.

A frown crossed Dex's face. "Old Man Ogden? That was years ago. Ten at least."

"Thirteen, actually," Josh corrected. "I was six-years-old and Agnes made me go to the wake."

Dex narrowed his eyes and nodded slowly. "You were scared of seeing your first body. I remember us talking out on the porch as we waited for Agnes to get ready. You wore that little suit of mine."

Despite the memory, Josh felt a warm rush at the

thought of having worn Dex's clothes, of having something that had been next to Dex's skin next to his as well.

"That's right. And we walked to the Ogden's house, trying to stay in the shade because it was so hot that day."

"Hotter than usual for spring." Dex's voice was quiet.

"The house was hot inside, too," Josh said, and he looked into the fire as he thought back to that day, that first time. "As we walked in, I felt it get even hotter. It scared me because it was like I'd eaten something hot and it wouldn't cool down, just kept heating up inside me."

"You got sick," Dex said. "I remember that now. You were sweating and pale, and something...happened." He frowned. "You started screaming."

Josh nodded and tried to stop the trembling inside him as he worked up the nerve to finally tell someone what he'd seen, what he had felt, all these years. He took a breath and fixed his gaze on Dex.

"It was worse when we walked up to the body. I thought I was on fire, I was so hot. I was sure it was what Hell feels like. Agnes had hold of my hand as we stood there talking to Ogden's wife and Old Man Ogden lay in the coffin in front of us.

"I stared at the body. I'd never seen one before, and I kept feeling more and more hot. And then, Old Man Ogden moved."

Dex narrowed his eyes. "What?"

Josh nodded and looked at Dex with wide eyes. "He moved. I swear to God, Dex, his fingers clenched. Ogden's daughter saw it, too, but she'd never admit to it. She's your age, I think, and was standing beside her mother but looking at her father's body and I saw her eyes widen and we looked at each other."

"That's why you ran outside," Dex said.

Another nod. "The heat was all inside me, like I'd swallowed fire, and I just had to get away. I screamed and pulled free of Agnes and ran outside where it felt so much cooler."

"I remember that now. I found you splashing water on your face at the pump." Dex was quiet a moment. "You were scared, and I walked you home."

Josh nodded, remembering how good it had felt to have his back to the Ogden house and Dex beside him. "I had nightmares for weeks after that. I kept dreaming that Old Man Ogden sat up and grabbed me, that he bit me as I screamed and kicked and punched at him." Josh shuddered. "That was the only time my whole life I was close to a body. Until this past week."

"What are you saying?" Dex asked.

"When I'm near a dead person, a heat starts inside of me." Josh swallowed past the words stuck in his throat. Now was the time to tell someone, to finally have it out. "And then the dead person... moves."

Josh studied Dex's handsome face in the firelight, watching for a reaction. But all he saw was Dex's eyes narrow slightly and his lips press together as he leaned closer over the table.

"Tell me," Dex finally said.

# FIFTEEN

While the fire burned and sunrise lightened the sky, Josh told Dex about Wayland and Agnes. He left nothing out, including the visit from Balthazar the night before and how the man had called the wolves to do his bidding.

When he finally finished, Josh looked up from the dying fire. The shadows had crowded around them as the fire had burned low, and Dex's expression was hidden.

When he did not speak, Josh cleared his throat and said in a voice that came out sounding colder than he had intended, "Go ahead, tell me I'm crazy. I know you want to."

Dex ran his hands over his face then turned to look into the fire. He was quiet for so long Josh was about to scream at him to say something, anything.

Then Dex finally looked at him and said in a low voice, "I don't think you're crazy, Josh."

Josh blinked. "You don't?"

"Nope."

"Truth?" It was what they used to say when they were young and something the other had said surprised them.

Dex grinned. "Truth. I'm not about to say I understand everything that happens in this world. And I've seen a lot of things myself the past few days that I can't explain. Hell, I've got Doc Brandt telling me I need to either drink more or less, he can't decide which." Dex took a breath. "As for Agnes, Doc and I both saw there was no blood where she'd been shot, and I saw the side table with the scratches in it."

Josh widened his eyes and pointed at Dex. "That was Agnes! She did that when she..." The excitement bled out of his voice and he cleared his throat, suddenly aware at how inappropriate he sounded. "When she came back."

Dex leaned toward him over the table. "I know what you did was real difficult —"

Josh shook his head and looked back into the fire. "Worst thing ever."

"And I believe everything you just told me. But..." When Dex paused, Josh looked up and saw him raise his eyebrows. "I don't know if other people are going to believe it."

Josh nodded. He was quiet a moment, thinking back over his time spent living with Agnes in town and how the sheriff and the townspeople had handled the law. He thought about the Indian they had caught trying to kidnap a young girl when he had been about ten. They had taken the Indian straight to a tree outside town and hung him. His body had stayed there for a week as a warning to the rest of the tribe until one morning they found it had been cut down, but no one ever knew who took it.

Josh thought that, although he wasn't an Indian, he was still seen as an outsider to some of the town because Agnes had taken him in after his mother had gone missing. His past was a mystery, and though Agnes had tried to shield him from it, he had heard the whispers as he grew up.

Some said that his mother had been a witch or a devil worshipper. Others believed his father had been a demon or, even an Indian. He understood his position in the town and knew that if they found out he had shot their beloved Agnes, no matter that she had already been dead, he would be ridden out to that same tree and hung. No trial, no chance to tell his side of it. He'd be choking and wiggling like that Indian while the rope dug into his throat and his eyes bulged out.

"Josh?"

He blinked and looked up. "Sorry. I was thinking about that Indian."

Dex frowned. "The one they hung out at the tree all those years ago?" Josh nodded, but Dex set his mouth and shook his head. "I will not let that happen."

Josh let out a humorless laugh. "Thanks, but I don't know if you and me can hold off the entire town."

"I think Sheriff Haden will listen to me," Dex said. "He's a good man."

"I shot Agnes and Wayland." Josh shook his head as he spoke the words, still amazed at what had happened. "People liked them. And I know what they used to say about me. Hell, what they still say. I won't get a trial, Dex. I won't get a chance to tell my side of it. They'll throw a rope over that tree limb and hang me, then laugh as I kick."

"Stop it!" Dex snapped. A heavy sadness had fallen over his face and he looked away into the fire. When he turned back, his lips were pressed tight together and his jaw was set in that stubborn way that was so very familiar.

"I won't let them just hang you. I can't lose you. I won't.

There are a lot of things happening in town lately. Strange things, difficult to explain, but I think they're all connected." He sighed and looked away. "They have to be."

Josh cocked his head. "What aren't you telling me?"

Dex took a breath. He was quiet a moment, long enough for Josh to reach across the short table and squeeze his wrist.

"Hey, Dex. Come on, I told you my crazy story. It's your turn now."

"Something happened last night at the Rooster. Something I can't explain. But your story about the stranger, what was his name?"

"Balthazar," Josh offered.

"Right. This Balthazar sounds very similar to how some of the girls from the Rooster were acting."

Dex told him the story, explaining also about what he found at the Overbrooke farm and his conversation with Doc Brandt. When he had finished, Dex pulled the cross on its chain from beneath his shirt and they both looked at it dangling between them in the firelight.

"My mother gave it to me on my thirteenth birthday," Dex said quietly.

"I remember," Josh said.

Dex smiled. "It belonged to my Pa, and she always said if he'd been wearing it that day he left to bring the cattle down from the mountains, he'd probably have returned." Dex shook his head and tucked the cross back inside his shirt. "Up until tonight I always thought it was just talk. But now, after how that girl reacted, I have to wonder."

Josh could see the firelight reflected in Dex's eyes and he reached out to squeeze his hand. A comfortable silence slid around them, filled with years of memories and trust.

"I'm sorry, Dex. I know this is tough for you, too. We'll get through it together, just like we used to get in trouble growing up, right?"

Dex gave a dry chuckle and turned back. They looked at each other in silence, the fire popping and crackling beside them. An excited flutter started in Josh's stomach as the expression on Dex's face changed, became more intense, charged with a sudden and dangerous attraction. With a stubborn will of its own, Josh's cock bloomed into life, hard in moments and confined painfully inside his breeches.

"Josh..."

Josh's breath was locked in his chest. "Yes?"

Dex half stood out of the chair and leaned over the table, now so close Josh could feel his breath on his cheek. Josh's cock throbbed as he stared into Dex's eyes and fought down the panic building inside him. What were they doing? This was Dex, his best friend and a sheriff's deputy, and Josh was an outlaw. If Sheriff Haden discovered Dex had found Josh and not taken him into custody, Dex could be hung alongside Josh as a traitor. And, foregoing all of that, what would it do to their friendship?

Without another word, Dex moved closer and kissed him. It was a light kiss, questioning, just a brush of Dex's lips against his own. But the feel of a man's mouth against his, the scratch of whiskers, the realization that it was Dex that kissed him—handsome, loyal, caring Dex—made Josh's head spin.

The kiss lasted just a moment, but when Dex leaned back they smiled at each other.

"I've wanted you to do that for years," Josh said.

Dex laughed and a blush rose in his cheeks. He looked away into the fire then back again, his grin showing off his dimples.

"I've wanted *you* to do that for years."

Josh smiled and leaned in for another kiss. This time there was no hesitation, no question if the kiss would be returned. They kissed for several minutes, mouths parting to admit the other's questing tongue. Josh's awareness narrowed to Dex's mouth: the heat and force of his tongue, the feel of Dex's teeth beneath his own tongue.

A sharp pop from the fire startled them both and they broke apart, staring at one another.

"This is dangerous, Dex," Josh said. "We shouldn't do this." But the words sounded like a lie, even to his own ears. His cock pulsed within his breeches, aching to be free. He could feel that it already leaked, weeping for release with Dex.

"I've wanted to be with you for too long to care about that now." Dex's voice was low and spiked with lust, the timbre of his words like a fist that wrapped around Josh's cock and squeezed.

Dex moved fast, standing and pulling him out of his chair, crushing his mouth over Josh's. Dex's tongue lunged past Josh's lips and filled his mouth, commanding, insistent. Dex's large, rough hands pulled Josh against him and the heat of Dex's body soaked into him, sinking in right to his bones, making him feel safe and loved.

They stretched out on the floor in front of the fire, Dex sprawled on top, his cock like a fence post pressed against Josh's thigh. The kiss that had started frantic slowed and deepened. Dex's fingers eased open the buttons of Josh's shirt as they kissed and when it lay open, Dex pulled the bottom of his linen undershirt out of his breeches. Sliding a hand beneath the soft fabric, Dex's fingers finally touched Josh's bare skin. He shivered at Dex's touch and pulled back to gasp.

Dex slid off Josh and furrowed his brow. "You all right?"

Josh felt himself blush and nodded as he smiled. "I'm all right. I just... I've never been touched that way before. It caught me by surprise is all."

Dex smiled and leaned down to kiss him again. "Me neither," he whispered.

They shoved aside the table and chairs and pulled the dusty quilt from the bed, spreading it on the floor by the fire. In moments they were nude, standing at either end of the quilt and staring at each other. A flurry of emotions whipped through Josh like a cyclone—lust, eagerness, nervousness, fear. He stared at the broad, hardened length of Dex's cock, the glistening head half hidden by foreskin, and thought how different it looked this way: more demanding and insistent.

"You're beautiful," Dex whispered.

Josh blushed and looked down, skimming his gaze over the firm, smooth planes of his torso, so different from Dex's broad chest and flat belly covered with fine dark hair.

"Come here," Dex said.

Looking up, Josh saw that Dex stood in the middle of the quilt, hand extended to him. Dex's dark brown nipples were hard and cast shadows across his chest in the firelight. The gold cross glittered where it lay nestled in the hair between.

Josh took Dex's hand and allowed himself to be drawn close. They embraced, arms around each other, lips together, tongues touching and rolling, learning the rhythm of the other. He felt Dex's hot, hard length press against his hip and Josh ground his own cock against him.

They lay down, stretching out along the soft quilt, the fire Dex had built warming them as they rolled and kissed.

Josh touched places he'd long fantasized about, gripping the solid shaft of Dex's cock, cupping his balls, clutching the rounded, hairy cheeks of his ass. And all the while they kissed, tasting each other as if they would never be able to get enough.

Dex rolled Josh onto his back and slid down, kissing and taking his nipples between his teeth. Josh closed his eyes and surrendered to Dex, moaning and gasping with each new place touched by his tongue. When Dex licked the length of Josh's cock, then moved up to take him into his mouth, Josh cried out in surprise and a blaze of desire.

"Oh God, Dex," Josh groaned. He closed his eyes and focused on Dex moving his mouth up and down the suddenly pulsing, bucking length of his cock as his climax gathered hot and powerful at the base of his spine. It shot forth, blasting into the damp, eager depths of Dex's throat where he swallowed it down.

Josh pulled Dex off him and kissed him deep, tasting the tang of his seed and hungry for Dex's. He rolled Dex onto his back and returned the favor, licking and kissing the hot skin of his cock, taking it in his mouth and tasting the sweat. This was Dex, the center of the man and pure masculine essence that made him who he was. This was a part of Dex no other person, man or woman, had ever known before.

"Oh, God," Dex groaned above him. "Josh... Oh, Josh. I'm gonna..."

Dex erupted in his mouth and Josh tried to swallow as much as he could, but a good portion of the thick, white seed spilled out from between his lips and ran down the sides of the shaft. When Dex had finished, Josh used his tongue to collect as much of the spilled stuff as he could, then crawled up over his body to lie in the crook of Dex's arm.

They kissed, tasting each other and themselves. The kiss deepened and, soon, both were hard again.

"Dex," Josh said between kisses. "I've thought about you so often."

"Me too," Dex said.

"I want you to..." Josh paused, unsure how to ask. It wasn't a natural act, but at this moment nothing in Belkin's Pass was natural. He kissed Dex again and said, "I want you inside me."

Dex rose up on an elbow and smiled down at him. The firelight sparked in the calm, blue lakes of Dex's eyes. "Are you sure?"

Josh licked his lips and nodded. "I am. I've heard men at the Rooster talk about it, and I've always wanted that with you. Just... Slowly."

They repositioned, Dex kneeling between Josh's legs. He took hold of Josh's feet and lifted his legs, hooking his ankles over the tops of his shoulders. Dex leaned down and ran the wide, soft top of his tongue up Josh's granite length, then moved lower and licked the sensitive, hairy globes of Josh's balls, nuzzling into the valley where his leg joined his torso.

"Oh, yeah," Josh gasped. "Right there."

But Dex did not linger. He used his tongue to paint his saliva lower still, coating the crack of Josh's ass and flicking the tip across the twitching button of Josh's hole. Josh closed his eyes, thought back on all the nights he had quietly worked a finger into himself, pushing to get at the spot that burned for a touch deep inside. Some nights he was able to find it, stroke it, press it, and send himself into shattering orgasm, biting back Dex's name behind clenched teeth.

And now Dex rose up between Josh's legs, drew a blunt, rough finger from between his lips. Josh felt the tip of Dex's finger circle the outside of his hole, wetting it, slicking it with spit, marking Josh as Dex's property. Dex dipped his finger inside, up to the first knuckle, retreated, dipped again, deeper, and continued to dip and retreat until he had one finger buried in him.

Josh groaned and squirmed beneath him. Dex added a second finger, keeping them tight together then spreading them apart, easing him open, preparing him. More spit pushed in deep by his fingers, Dex worked patiently as the fire crackled beside them and dawn lightened the windows.

Finally, Dex took his swollen length in hand, spread the beads of slick, silvery juice around the rounded crown of his cock and pressed it to Josh's hole. Dex took hold of Josh's ankles and, locking his gaze on Josh's face, eased into him.

Josh felt the rugged ring of his entrance resist at first, but Dex persisted and, soon, the broad tip pushed past. An uncomfortable burning followed, but Josh focused instead on relaxing his muscles around the burrowing pole.

"You grip me so tight," Dex grunted. He paused to close his eyes and catch his breath and when he opened them, they looked at each other a long moment.

"I love you," Dex said.

Josh lifted up and Dex leaned down to meet him for a kiss.

"I love you," Josh replied.

Dex kissed him again, then straightened up and pushed the rest of the way inside. He pulled back and pushed in slowly, picking up speed until he was plunging into Josh with deep thrusts. Each stroke sent Dex's cock across the magic spot Josh had worked so hard to get to on his own and, in minutes, he felt himself spill over the edge and reached down to stroke himself to a splattering climax.

His muscles tightened around Dex's invading cock, gripping it hard, and he soon followed suit. With a shout and a shudder, Dex tipped back his head and plunged in deep, his hips convulsing as he pumped his seed within Josh's most intimate of places.

Sweat rolled down Dex's face and torso and Josh winced at the sting of Dex's withdrawal. Dex used a corner of the ratty old quilt to wipe them both clean, then stretched out alongside Josh, smiling and leaning in for a kiss. Josh closed his eyes and waited, but when the expected kiss didn't happen, Josh opened his eyes.

Dex supported himself with one arm beside him, eyes open and looking off toward the door, his expression troubled.

"What is it?" Josh asked.

"Heard something."

Josh held his breath and looked away from the distraction of Dex's handsome face to listen as well. The distant sound of a number of horses came to him and a cold flood of fear ran through him.

He cut his eyes back to Dex just as the man pushed up to his feet and crossed to the window, his bare feet making padding sounds on the old wood floor. Josh scrambled up from the floor and, shivering, joined Dex to peer through the cloudy glass. The sun had risen over the prairie, the pink of sunrise fading into yellow. The land stretched away, empty and vast, leading back to town.

"See 'em?" Josh asked.

"Nope. But they're comin'," Dex whispered. He looked at Josh. "Quite a few of 'em, too. Sheriff and some other men from town would be my guess."

Josh tried to swallow but something felt as if it were

lodged in his throat. He couldn't seem to get enough air and started to feel dizzy. Stumbling back against the table, he pulled out a chair and sank into it. Drawing in a shaky breath, Josh looked at Dex.

"They'll hang me, Dex."

Dex crossed and knelt between his legs, hands on his knees. The cross bounced against his bare chest, winking in the sunlight. "Let me talk to them."

"But then they'll hang you, too."

"Sheriff Haden knows me," Dex assured him. "He'll listen to me."

"I can't die knowing you're dying because of me," Josh said as tears blurred his vision. He stubbornly wiped them away with the back of his hand. "Not now, when we've finally been able to be together."

Dex stood and kissed him, a hand on the side of his face. When he pulled back, Josh could see tears in Dex's eyes as well and his stomach knotted even tighter.

"Let me go out and talk to them. I'll ride up the road a piece and try to get them to turn back. I'll tell Sheriff Haden you'll let me bring you in at night with no one else around."

Fear closed Josh's throat so that all he could do was nod. Dex kissed him again, quickly, and got up. He moved around the small house, gathering his clothes.

Josh followed suit, watching as Dex sat in a chair to pull on his boots, then got up, the heels of his boots loud against the old wood floor as he shrugged into his coat and grabbed his hat. Dex opened the door, glanced back once to smile at Josh where he stood by the fire buttoning his shirt, then stepped outside and pulled the door closed after him.

CHAPTER

# SIXTEEN

Dex saw them the moment he hit the main road. A long line of men, ten at least, with Sheriff Haden leading the way. The sheriff sat tall in his saddle, reins clutched tight in his hands. The sun was high enough now to throw all of the men's faces into shadow, and for a moment Dex could almost imagine them all ghosts heading back to their haunts after a long night scaring the townspeople.

He urged his horse to a trot and caught them half a mile from the abandoned house. Sheriff Haden held up a hand as he reined in his horse and the men following him came to an obedient stop.

"Sheriff, you must have got back early."

"Deputy," the sheriff said with a nod. "I came in just after sun up and got an earful from Doc Brandt and a few others. Looks like you've been out here pretty much all night. What brings you out to these parts?"

"I was lookin' for Josh Stanton," Dex replied. "Same as you all, I guess." He met the eye of every man in the group, establishing a connection with each to hopefully remind

128

them that they trusted him as the law in town right after the sheriff.

"That's right, we're lookin' for him," a younger man shouted from the back of the group and Dex picked out Grant Olsen, oldest son of Holden Olsen, the town carpenter. "He killed Agnes Pritchett. There's a bounty on his head."

"And Wayland Overbrooke!" someone else added.

"You don't know that," Dex replied, trying to keep his voice even.

"Got a witness saw him shoot Agnes, Dex," Sheriff Haden said, his voice calm, hands folded over his saddle horn. "And you know that."

"I know Ling Chen said she saw someone shoot Agnes," Dex said, "but it was dark in the house, and the wind was up, throwin' sand."

The sheriff shook his head and eased his horse up closer to Dex. When Grant Olsen tried to move up as well, Sheriff Haden stopped him with a look, then turned back to Dex.

"What's goin' on out here, deputy?"

Dex lowered his voice and leaned in over the saddle horn. "Sheriff, you can't just ride up and take him. Josh loved Agnes, you know that."

"I know that Agnes opened her house to a bastard child found sitting outside that house over there, his mother gone to Lord knows where and leaving him on his own." The sheriff flicked his eyes toward the house then brought them back to Dex. "I know that Agnes raised him as right as she could, what with no man to help her. And I know that a scared young girl watched through the window as that same child, that same fatherless welp Sheriff Dooley brought back to town and released to Agnes, repaid her years of upbringing by shooting her not once, but three times." Sheriff Haden sat up tall in his saddle and narrowed his eyes at Dex. "Now, you tell me, deputy, why I can't just ride up there and take him to the hangin' tree?"

"That's not how the law works, sheriff, and you know it."

"It's how the law works when I've got a witness who saw him pull the trigger."

"Sheriff, there's strange things happening in town these days," Dex said in a low voice, thinking about the way the saloon girls had attacked him. "I would think you could at least give Josh a chance to tell his side in court."

"There ain't anything strange going on now that I'm back from my visit," Sheriff Haden snapped. "And if you think I want to give that murderer a chance to fill our court with his lies, then you don't know me at all."

Dex had just opened his mouth to reply when Grant Olsen jabbed a thick finger out over the flat prairie land and said, "There he goes! That's 'im, ridin' away!"

Twisting in his saddle, Dex watched a cloud of dust make its way out from the barn where Josh had stabled his horse. "Dammit," Dex said beneath his breath as his heart lurched.

"Let's get him!" one of the men shouted.

"Hold it!" Sheriff Haden held up a hand. The men behind him grumbled but stayed where they were, horses stomping as if they, too, were itching to give chase. "He's heading out into Venom Valley."

Dex's gut twisted at the words and he realized Haden was right. Josh was heading straight for the long, flat stretch of desert prairie where nothing lived but snakes, scorpions, and wolves. Anyone who ventured too deep into Venom Valley had never been heard from again.

"He'll get away," one of the men whined.

"No," Haden replied. "He'll not be escaping his Fate in the valley. He'll get what's coming to him there." The sheriff lowered his voice and leaned toward Dex. "I get the feeling you've been consorting with a fugitive of the law, deputy. If I were to find out that's the case, I could hang you alongside or instead of him."

Dex nodded and the cold look in the sheriff's eyes kept him silent, unsure what he could say to make things right. He was caught between the man he loved and his duty as a deputy.

"I'll give you till noon tomorrow to bring him in from the valley," Sheriff Haden said as he reined his horse around and turned to look at Dex over his shoulder. "If you ain't back in town by then with Josh Stanton in tow, you might as well stay and take your chances in the valley."

Dex sat on his horse and watched the group ride off. A few of the men glanced over their shoulders at the fading cloud of dust that marked Josh's path, their mouths curved down with regret. There would be no hanging today.

He watched them go a bit longer, wishing he could just follow along behind, back to the only place and people he had known his whole life. But then he turned to watch the plume of dust from Josh's escape. How could he leave Josh to face Venom Valley on his own? After finally being honest with Josh, being intimate with him, he couldn't just turn his back on him. What kind of man would he be if he allowed his friend, his love, to ride off alone into the very heart of death?

There was nothing left for him back in town if Josh wasn't there. And even if he tried to just return to town now, Sheriff Haden would take the star from his chest, at the very least. Or hang him, if the mood in town had turned sour.

Pulling on the reins to bring his horse around to face Venom Valley, Dex clucked his tongue and said, "Come on, boy, let's go."

# SEVENTEEN

Josh had a fuzzy recollection of what his mother had looked like. She lived in his mind, ageless, warm, and loving, her long blond hair knotted in a single braid down her back, her blue eyes clear and hands rough from housework. She had laughed a lot, cooked hearty meals, and managed the few animals they had owned.

From what Josh could remember of the night his mother had vanished, there had been no moon. He had been at most five-years-old, but he could recall very well standing in the doorway of their house, digging his tiny nails into the wood as he clung to the doorframe and peered out into the dark, endless night, waiting for her to come back.

It had started with a great crash from the road. The sound had startled them both, he remembered that as well. His mother had pulled on a coat and stepped outside, face turned toward the dark stretch of road as a chill autumn wind pushed into the house and fluttered the candles. She stood very still a moment, watching and listening to the dark, then turned and told him to stay in the house.

It had been the last words she had ever said to him.

He didn't remember much after that. He supposed he had fallen asleep in the bed that they shared, pushed up in the corner of the room. Hours later he had awakened. It was daylight and he was hungry, but his mother had not been in the house.

A terror that grew with each step pushed him into a run, he remembered that. The feeling had gnawed at him like hunger, only colder. He had cried and screamed for her, running outside into the early morning light with no coat or boots. The cold, hard ground bit into the tender flesh of his feet as he had run to the barn calling for her.

But his mother was nowhere to be found.

From what Agnes told him, the sheriff at that time, a good man named Dooley, rode up the track to the house hours later and found Josh lying on his side on the ground, shivering, with his thumb in his mouth. Sheriff Dooley had ridden out that way to check on reports of what had sounded like a stagecoach crash the night before, and, sure enough, he had found the coach overturned in the ditch just past the end of the track that led to the house where Josh and his mother had lived. The horses were both dead, necks broken, and the coach was empty of cargo. Josh had overheard rumors over the years that the drivers had bite marks in their necks and their bodies had been drained of blood.

Dex had tried to console him through the years by calling the rumors of his mother's disappearance tall tales made up by idle minds. But Josh had heard the talk all over town, making it impossible to ignore. *Injuns*, some used to say. *Witchcraft*, others had said, and crossed themselves before scurrying away.

A rattler slid in front of Clementine, startling the horse

so she reared up and jerked him out of his thoughts. He kept himself in the saddle, barely, and soothed Clem as he guided her away from the snake. He eyed the thing warily, guessing it to be at least eight feet long. The rattler continued on, leaving its scaly print on the dusty dirt.

"Welcome to Venom Valley, girl," Josh whispered as he patted the horse's neck. Clem snorted and shook her head as if telling him this was a dangerous path, but she kept going.

Josh had ridden hard away from the house where he and Dex had spent the last half of the night, thoughts of the man rushing through his mind—the heat of Dex's kiss, the smell of his sweat, the taste of his flesh and seed, the feel of Dex's full length easing into him. The memories made him hard even as he raced his horse across the open land, fleeing for his life.

Venom Valley was more a shallow canyon, wedged between the rocky sides of two mountains that rose up from the prairie with sudden, granite force. The slopes of the mountains eased into grassland farther up, fed by snow-melt streams that made it perfect land for grazing animals. Many ranchers herded their sheep or cattle up the slopes, risking the rocky paths and the few miles of prairie desert valley floor they had to travel before making their way up to higher ground.

Hard packed dirt made up the floor of the valley, flooding with the spring rains that forced the deadly things that lived there to scuttle, crawl, and slither from their hiding spots. Scorpions, snakes, and stinging beetles made the valley their home, an unusual number of poisonous things that had earned the long stretch of land its name. Most folks would rather travel an extra day or two by circling around either mountain, or even risk their horse, or themselves, breaking a leg by attempting the rocky mountain paths rather than journey through the valley itself.

Some said the place was haunted, claiming to have heard horrible screams in the night that echoed from the many caves in the rocky cliff walls. Years ago, shortly after Josh's mother had vanished, a new arrival in town had found some gold nuggets in a stream deep inside the valley. The man had staked a claim and hired some outsiders to dig a mine in the rocky cliff walls. No one really knew what happened, but a few months later Josh could still recall Sheriff Dooley's pale face as he rode slowly back into town from checking on the miners. The town hadn't seen anyone from the mine for a couple weeks and when the sheriff got out there, the men were all dead, bodies scattered around inside the mine, mouths stretched wide in frozen screams.

Since the men were outsiders, they weren't to be buried in Belkin's Pass cemetery. Instead, the local preacher, Father Thomas, rode out with a group of men and boarded up the mine entrance, leaving the bodies where they lay inside. The preacher read a blessing when they were done, and they all rode back to town before nightfall. No one laid claim to the mine after that; no amount of gold was worth dying like that.

And now, Josh rode into the sun rising swiftly overhead, making his way into the only place around he knew no one would follow.

He pulled on the reins and brought Clementine to a halt. The mare shifted and snorted nervously, her eyes rolling as she shook her head. Josh patted her neck and scratched between her ears, a trick that usually calmed her down. It worked, somewhat, and he slid out of the saddle to stretch his sore muscles and drink from his water skin.

The valley was still and quiet, as if waiting for something

to happen. He shielded his eyes against the sun and peered up into the dark blue sky. Vultures circled high above, watching his progress through Venom Valley or keeping an eye on an animal struggling somewhere close by. Josh shuddered at the thought of their hooked beaks tearing into his flesh and looked away. He lifted the water skin for another sip and glanced back along the path he had ridden.

A tremble of fear passed through him at the sight of a small cloud of dust in the distance.

He was being pursued, even out here in Venom Valley.

He stoppered the water skin and tucked it away. Climbing into the saddle, he kicked Clem into a fast run. Visions flashed in his mind of a group of men from town running him down and putting a bullet in his head, or, worse, shooting him in the knees and leaving him squirming in the dirt for the vultures and other scavengers.

Clem ran fast, but she'd been running a long time. Quick glances behind proved his pursuers were riding just as hard. The dust cloud grew and, as he watched, the image of a lone rider became clear. He wasn't being pursued by a group, but rather a single horseman. Could it be Dex? Was he riding after him to take him back into town? Even though they had lain together last night, Josh wondered if Dex would turn his back on his oath to uphold the law in Belkin's Pass.

Letting out his breath, Josh eased Clem down to a trot, and then a walk. He watched over his shoulder as the rider approached. In the moments before he was able to make out the man's face, Josh felt a trembling uncertainty shake him. What if this wasn't Dex? What if this was Sheriff Haden, ready to arrest him for murdering Agnes and Wayland? Or, perhaps worse yet, what if it was Balthazar, the quietly menacing stranger from the night before?

Whoever the rider was, he was coming up fast, and Josh lifted his chin and turned Clem to face their pursuer. Whoever had followed him into such dangerous territory, Josh hoped it was Dex, his one chance for redemption and, if he dared to believe it, love.

# EIGHTEEN

A mix of emotions and a lifetime of memories rushed through Dex as he pushed Nightshade fast across the wasted lands of Venom Valley. Memories of Josh slipped through his mind—laughing with him during dinners at Agnes's table, the pale cheeks of his ass when they had swum in the creek, camping beneath the unending night sky with a small fire slowly dying beside them.

Dex could feel once again the hunger in Josh's kiss, taste the sharp spice of his seed, feel the damp, hot clench of Josh's body grabbing his cock, claiming him, owning him. It didn't feel real. Moe like one of the countless dreams and fantasies he had spun over the years. Just an incredibly vivid imaging of what it would be like to ease inside Josh, finally couple with him, lose himself inside the man he had fallen in love with so long ago.

But, no. It had actually happened. They had been together, had declared their love for each other.

And now Josh was on the run. Running from him and fleeing into the most dangerous part of land for miles around.

He had left Dex behind as he had escaped into Venom Valley, and anger warred with love inside him as he rode hard after Josh. What the fuck was Josh thinking? He would not last a day here in the valley.

Deep down, Dex knew he would not be returning to town. Everything he had ever known, his mother, the people he had grown up with, were left behind. He was leaving all of that behind to be with Josh.

It was a decision Dex had made before Josh had run. He'd wanted to do it in a more gradual manner, to allow him to get some personal effects, maybe leave his deputy position in a better manner. But circumstances had changed, changed in such a bad and dangerous way, and it was done now. There was no way to go back. He just wished he'd been able to see his mother one last time and explain his decision.

The sun hung high in the sky; daylight was quickly slipping away. The valley floor stretched out before him, dirt the color of autumn wheat. Around him, the mountains glowed in the sunlight, coming together in the hazy distance at the end of Venom Valley. Once he and Josh reached those mountains, the only way out was either a steep climb straight up the cliff walls or through a narrow, rocky path dark with misty shadows. Beyond the mountains stretched the prairie, open land as far as the eye could see, reaching all the way to California. They could ride for days without seeing another soul, sleep out beneath the stars and make love by the fire, the night winds cooling the sweat on their bare skin.

Turning his mind from a future he hoped they would both live to see, Dex focused on the sight of Josh and Clementine ahead of him. The fist of anxiety in his gut eased a bit when he realized Josh had reined his horse to a stop and turned to face him.

The thought of standing beside Josh, free to kiss him, touch him, taste the sweat on his skin, once again push his cock into Josh's soft depths, made Dex hard. He hunkered low over Nightshade and urged him faster.

Soon, Dex slowed Nightshade to a trot and then reined him in as he pulled up beside Josh where he sat astride Clementine. They looked at each other in silence a moment, facing opposite directions, the horses snorting and tossing their heads.

"Are you trying to kill yourself?" Dex said, his voice sharper than intended.

A flush colored Josh's cheeks and he looked away toward the mountains. "You didn't have to come after me. I know how to survive on my own."

Dex silently cursed himself and took a calming breath. "I know you do. But Venom Valley is dangerous. And with this Balthazar out there somewhere, and your reaction to dead bodies, you shouldn't be alone."

Josh snapped his head around to glare at Dex. "I'm not a child, Dex. I can take care of myself."

"I know that, but, dammit, don't you see?" Dex walked Nightshade closer and reached out to pull Josh forward into a kiss. When they broke apart, Dex kept his hand on the back of Josh's neck and looked into his eyes. "I love you, Josh Stanton. And I want to stand beside you from here on out, understand?"

Josh took a shaky breath and reached up to hang onto Dex's wrist. "You shouldn't have followed me."

"I couldn't let you ride out here alone." Dex looked around at the flat, dusty land between the mountain walls. "No one should be out here alone."

"How will you explain this to Sheriff Haden? You'll lose your job as deputy at least, most likely be hung next to me."

Dex looked back into Josh's eyes. "I'm not going back to town. We're in this together now, and we'll find out what's going on. Together."

"Dex, I can't ask that of you," Josh said.

"You didn't." Dex slid out of the saddle and stretched his back. He reached inside his coat and plucked the silver deputy star from his shirt.

"Are you sure?" Josh asked. "Are you really sure?"

Dex held the star in the palm of his hand, weighing it a moment as he stared at it. Sunlight glared off its surface, making him squint. Setting his jaw, Dex pulled his hand back and flung the star out into the flat, dry land. The sun winked off the star once, then it was lost to sight and he let out a breath.

Turning, he looked around the flat, dry valley, then up along the tops of the cliff walls before finally facing Josh again.

"There used to be a stream out this way. Near where they tried to have a go at the mine."

Josh dropped to the ground and reached out to put a comforting hand on his shoulder. They stood in silence a moment, then Josh released him and looked around as well.

"I remember hearing about that mine. Was it this far out?"

"Yep." Dex looked at Josh. "Made it tough for anyone to ride into town and back before nightfall. Had to run the shoes right off a horse to get there and back safely."

"How far, do you know?"

"Another few miles, maybe a bit farther."

"Think we can make the mine before nightfall?"

"Maybe. Might have to push the horses a little more." Dex stretched again. "From what I heard there were some buildings around the boarded up mine. Offices, bunkers for the miners, things like that."

"We'll need to water the horses soon, but let's give it a try. I'd feel better with some kind of shelter out here at night."

"Right about that," Dex replied.

They saddled up and rode on toward the distant mountains as the sun wheeled overhead. Sometime later, just as the sun began to dip down toward the mountains ahead of them, they came upon a narrow stream fed by a runoff of water tumbling over the top of the cliff. They dismounted and pulled the saddles and bridles off their horses and let the animals drink.

Kneeling upstream of the horses, they washed the dirt from their hands, faces, and the backs of their necks, then drank their fill from cupped hands. The water was cold and Dex's fingers were numb by the time he stood up.

"Let's have a look around," he said and stepped across the stream in time with Josh to walk along the side of the cliff.

Around a pile of boulders they found a small, tumble-down shack, a long bunker where the miners had slept, and, just beyond that, the boarded up entrance to the mine. The boards were weathered and dry from exposure to the elements. Gaps had formed between some of them and rodents and other critters had pulled apart the lower boards to gain access. The gaps in the boards allowed damp, chill air from the depths of the mine to slip out over the valley.

"Can't imagine dying in there," Dex whispered. He stepped up to the boarded entrance and squinted between a gap, trying to see deeper into the darkness. The sun was just past the point of shining into the mine entrance and provided no further illumination. Turning, he looked around to find Josh standing back by the weather beaten shack, arms folded over his chest, eyes wide in his pale face.

"What's wrong?" Dex asked, walking up to stand beside him.

"I felt... something."

"Something?"

Josh turned his gaze to Dex and in his wide brown eyes Dex could see Josh was truly frightened. "It's hard to explain," Josh said. "It feels as though my blood is... boiling. I start to feel warm inside, and it gets hotter and hotter. That's what I felt out at Wayland's farm, and then I walked into his barn and saw him standing there, eating that chicken. And then when I found Agnes a few days later, I felt the same thing."

Dex looked at the boarded up mine entrance, then back at Josh. "You think when you get close to a dead body you start to... affect it?"

Josh sighed and dropped to his butt on the ground. He rested his wrists on his upraised knees and hung his head. "I don't know, Dex. I just know what I felt three times before, and each of those times someone dead has moved, and two of them got up and attacked me." He lifted his head and stared at the mine entrance. "And if all the stories I've heard about that mine are true, I don't want to get any closer to it."

Sitting in the dirt beside Josh, Dex reached out and placed a hand on the back of his neck. "I can assure you that the story we heard about that mine growing up was true. Sheriff Dooley found all forty miners plus the cook and the foreman just inside the entrance. They were all dead with looks of terror frozen on their faces." Dex felt Josh shudder beneath his hand, and leaned in closer. "The thing they never told anyone else but I found in Sheriff Dooley's log was, it seemed they had all been drained of blood as well."

Josh jerked his head around and looked up at Dex. "Truth?"

Dex gave him a short, grim nod and leaned back. "Truth." He rubbed the back of Josh's neck a moment longer then got to his feet. "And from what I saw at the Rooster last night, I wouldn't be surprised." He brushed dirt from his hands and reached down to help Josh to his feet. "Come on, let's gather firewood and set up camp."

"Dex?" Josh said as Dex turned away, and the man faced him again. "Thanks for coming after me. And for believing me."

Dex took Josh's face between his palms and searched his dark brown eyes. "You're welcome." He kissed him, flicking the tip of his tongue across Josh's lips before stepping back. "We'd best get to work, or we won't have a fire come sundown."

# NINETEEN

Night was fast laying claim to the valley, and Dex was glad Josh had found a small scrub tree that had been hollowed out by insects. He worked with flints to get a fire going as Josh spread their bed rolls between the fire and the old shack. They had decided to stay outside as long as possible and retreat to the shack after nightfall. As the horses snuffled nearby for prairie grass, they stretched out alongside each other.

"Red sky at night, we all sleep tight," Josh said, staring up at the red-stained clouds. Dex could hear a nervous hitch in Josh's voice and understood exactly how he felt.

"Red sky at morning, we all heed the warning," Dex finished. He rolled on his side and looked at Josh's profile before the fire. "My Pa taught me that, too."

Josh turned his head to look at him. Firelight sparked in tears in his eyes. "Agnes taught it to me."

Moving slowly, being careful not to spook him, Dex leaned in and kissed him. It was a soft kiss, still unfamiliar and exciting. It quickly deepened, and Dex heard Josh moan low in his chest. Dex slid closer, the bedroll wrinkling beneath him. He hooked a leg over Josh's, slid it up Josh's thigh until the top of his knee pressed into the warmth of Josh's crotch.

He unbuttoned Josh's shirt, spread the material apart to expose the undershirt. Running his hand down Josh's torso, he felt the muscles of his belly tremble beneath the material, and he grabbed a fistful of the soft material to pull the tail of the undershirt from inside Josh's breeches. Josh gasped up into Dex's mouth when his hand touched bare skin.

Josh broke their kiss and turned away, hiding an embarrassed smile behind his hand. He looked back at Dex after a moment.

"Sorry. I'm just not used to being touched by you. Like that."

"Not yet." Dex leaned down to kiss him again, filling Josh's mouth with his tongue. He slid his hand beneath the undershirt and up along fevered skin to Josh's chest. Still kissing, Dex rolled Josh's nipple between his fingers until it hardened. He flicked the nub a few times, earning moans and quiet gasps from Josh, then moved to the other one.

Josh pushed Dex away and sat up. His eyes glittered with passion as he peeled off his shirts and pulled off his boots. Dex followed Josh's lead, and a few breaths later both stood nude before the fire. The sky darkened toward full night and a few stars appeared, blinking shyly down on them. The moon had not yet risen, but Dex could see its cold glow in the dark blue of the coming night, just over the mountains on the other side of the valley.

"You're beautiful," Dex said.

"Not as beautiful as you," Josh replied. He stepped

forward into Dex's embrace, their cocks jousting briefly and their arms going around each other.

Dex broke the kiss this time to sit on the bedroll and pull Josh into his lap. They kissed some more, then Josh positioned himself with his legs to either side of Dex's torso, their cocks pressed together against Dex's belly. The slick of their combined juices tangled in the dark hair on his stomach.

"I want you inside me again," Josh said between kisses. "I can't stop thinking about it."

Dex needed no further encouragement. He gathered the beads of slick from each of their cocks and used it to work a finger inside Josh as he sat on Dex's lap. He kissed Josh as he fingered him, their moans echoing off the rock wall rising just beyond the shack over Dex's shoulder.

When he felt Josh was ready, Dex collected more of the slick from the both of them and covered his cock with it. The length throbbed in his grip, pulsing and hot.

Josh lifted up and Dex leaned back on his elbows. He watched Josh spit into his palm several times, then reach back to take him in hand. The touch of Josh's hand shot through him, and Dex trembled. Josh spread the spit along him, adjusted his position, and slowly sat down. The tight band of muscle resisted a moment, but then Dex felt his foreskin push back and the smooth, round head, slick with juice, eased inside.

Josh closed his eyes and braced himself with his arms to either side of Dex. He took his time and Dex let him move at his own pace, content to lean back and watch his friend now turned lover slowly seat himself. Soon enough, Josh sat fully impaled, head tipped back and mouth open to fill up with starlight. Josh's cock jutted out toward Dex, glistening strings of juice dripping onto Dex's belly.

The movement in Josh's hips started slow but hurriedly gathered speed. Dex lay flat and closed his eyes, feeling the hot, slick push and retreat, the wet grip of Josh's body, and press of Josh's thighs against him.

His attention sharpened and narrowed to the tingle that started in the very tip of his cock. It sparked and caught, rushing through him to grab his balls and the base of his spine in a fist made of lightning. Then Dex heard himself shout, felt his hips lift from the bedroll to thrust himself deep into Josh as his seed surged out of him.

Moments later, Josh ground his hips down, pushing Dex deeper still, and Josh took hold of himself. He gave three quick strokes and a slick ribbon of come landed on Dex's face. The rest puddled on Dex's chest and belly, and Dex wiped up what he could find and greedily sucked his fingers clean.

Josh leaned forward to press their foreheads together, breath hot on Dex's face. They stayed that way, Dex's softening cock still inside Josh, each of them catching their breath.

Then Josh sighed and, after a soft kiss, whispered, "You have made a man of me, Dexter Wells," before he lifted his hips and allowed Dex's cock to slap down against his own belly.

"And you have done the same for me," Dex replied.

They pulled on their boots, mindful of rattlers and scorpions, and Dex grabbed the end of a burning branch to light their way to the stream where they cleaned up in the cold, clear water. Thoroughly chilled, they hurried back to the fire and cuddled together beneath a bedroll to look at the stars and watch the point of the quarter moon peek over the mountain. The valley lightened around them beneath the moon's glow, and Dex felt Josh's body tense in his arms.

"What is it?" Dex asked, his senses sharpening and muscles tensing as well.

"I saw something."

"Where?"

"Out in the valley, half a mile."

Dex squinted, straining his eyes, but saw nothing. "What did it look like?"

Josh's voice shook. "A wolf."

Clementine snorted from the darkness, tied up just out of sight of where they lay around a corner of the cliff. She snorted again, then let out a startled bray. Nightshade followed suit and Dex's heart, so calm only moments before, lurched in fear.

"Get dressed," Dex whispered. "Fast."

# TWENTY

Josh kept his back to the rough, weathered boards of the old shack as he pulled on his breeches and slid his arms into his shirts. He moved his gaze back and forth across the moonlit valley floor, trying to find the movement again. The deep shadows seemed to move in the still, quiet chill of the evening, mocking him.

He pushed his feet into his boots, and then stood straight up, a bolt of fear running through him as the horses brayed even louder. The sound of both horses rearing up and pawing at the ground came out of the darkness and, just as Dex pulled his gun from the holster, the horses galloped away from them and out into the valley. The moonlight gleamed on the muscles across their backs and down their legs as they fled.

Two sleek, shadowed shapes pursued the horses for several yards until Dex let out a loud, piercing whistle that made Josh jump. Josh watched, wide-eyed and panting, as the wolves stopped to look back at them.

"Oh shit," Dex whispered.

"How many bullets do you have?" Josh asked.

"Six loaded. Twelve in my belt. We'll be fine."

The two wolves slowly approached. Their large heads hung low as if too heavy for their necks. White moonlight bleached their dark fur as it rippled across muscled shoulders. Each paw was as big as Dex's fist.

"It's okay," Dex assured Josh without taking his eyes off the wolves. He adjusted his grip on the gun and both of them instinctively took a few steps back until they were pressed up against the shack.

"I'm getting a branch and my rifle," Josh whispered. Before Dex could say anything, Josh darted forward, stomping over the bedroll where they had just made love. He grabbed the stock of his rifle and stretched out a hand to take hold of the cool end of a burning branch.

As he lifted the torch over his head, the fire cast a wide arc of golden light and dozens of pairs of eyes reflected back the glow. Josh's balls pulled up and his breath stopped in his chest as an icy chill shot up his spine.

"Fuck it all," Dex said, and Josh knew he had seen as well.

Josh backed up to stand beside Dex and laid the branch on the ground to chamber a round in his rifle. "How many?"

"A dozen. Probably more." Dex took a step forward and shouted, waving his hands. The wolves paused for the barest moment, then continued their slow advance.

"Can we take them all?" Josh asked as he picked up the burning branch.

"Not all of them," Dex said. "Not fast enough."

Josh backed up against the shack and the door on the side facing the mine rattled in its frame. He looked around at the shack, turned back to look at the advancing wolves, then grabbed Dex's arm and stepped to the side of the structure.

"Hey!" Dex said, keeping an eye on the wolves. "What are you doing?"

"In here," Josh explained as he pushed open the door and stepped into the shack. An agitated rattle stopped him in his tracks and they both jumped back just before the snake struck. The door swung shut, trapping the snake inside, and Dex grabbed Josh by the arm and pulled him toward the mine.

Waves of heat rushed through Josh's system as they approached the mine, making him dizzy and he stumbled. He yanked his arm from Dex's grip.

Dex spun to glare at him. "What are you doing?"

"I can't go near the mine!" Josh shouted and dropped to his knees. He felt his grip loosen on the rifle and torch as the strange heat washed through him. This heat was worse than it had been with Wayland and Agnes. It was as if the fire inside him had been multiplied a thousand times. As he knelt in the sand with his back to the wolves, his blood felt as if were already boiling.

"Josh!" Dex knelt in front of him and grabbed his shoulders. He gave Josh a rough shake but he could not focus. All he knew, all he could feel, was the heated rush of his blood.

Dex pulled Josh against him, hugging him against his chest. As if through a wall of rushing sound, Josh heard the crack of Dex's Colt and felt the jump of the man's shoulder as Dex held off the wolves. Then Dex had his hands under Josh's arms and was dragging him across the hard packed sand and dirt to the mine entrance. Josh tried to speak, tried to warn Dex not to get any closer, but his tongue was hot and swollen behind his teeth.

Josh felt himself spin around, and then Dex had sat him up against the weathered and rotting boards that covered the old mine entrance. Cool, dank air washed over him, bringing with it a hint of things left too long in the dampness. The air chilled his fevered, sweaty skin, and Josh shivered. His senses returned a little and he watched Dex kneeling before him, protecting him, waving the burning branch at the advancing wolves as he shouted. Dex was saving his bullets, Josh knew, for when the wolves were close enough for them to feel their breath.

Soft, skittering sounds whispered out of the mine. Shuffling, crackling sounds that sent a familiar chill through him. Someone, *something*, was moving behind the rotting boards that covered the mine entrance. Josh slowly turned his head, the rugged, splintered surface of the board beneath catching in his sweat-damp hair.

A face with skin dry as parchment hovered just on the other side of a gap in the boards. Rotted teeth stuck up from brown gums and a milky white eye rolled to meet Josh's gaze. The thing let out a rank gasp of air as it moaned and stuck skeletal fingers through the narrow gap, the tips brushing along Josh's cheek.

He gave a start, the touch of the thing snapping him from his daze even as the heat in his body burned hotter. More fingers from other walking corpses reached out for him, and Josh pushed away from the boards that covered the mine, letting out a shout of fear. As he watched, a number of bone thin hands gripped the edges of the boards and pulled the rotted wood apart, making a path for the revived dead miners to shuffle out toward them.

CHAPTER

# TWENTY-ONE

The wolves crept closer.

Dex waved the burning branch and shouted, but the beasts were getting more brazen.

One medium sized wolf lunged. Dex put a bullet in its head. It dropped hard to the ground, its gleaming teeth less than a foot from the toe of Dex's boot. He was down to four bullets in his gun with no time to reload. He had to make each bullet count.

And then Josh gave a terrified shout behind him.

Dex's heart jumped, and he glanced over his shoulder, still waving the burning branch at the wolves in front of him. He expected to see a wolf, maybe two, that had snuck around and up on them from their blind side.

What he saw stopped him in his tracks. Cold fingers of dread rattled up the length of his spine and, for a brief second, the wolves were forgotten.

A space had been torn open in the boards that covered the mine. Shuffling out of that ragged opening came men dressed in the tattered overalls and shirts of miners. They were not living, nor could Dex think of them as dead, seeing as how they were walking and advancing on Josh.

A snarl and snap from in front of him brought Dex back to the wolves. He turned away from the miners and thrust the burning branch at the nearest wolf. The flame sizzled against the side of the large jaws, and the wolf yelped and jumped back.

"Dex!" Josh shouted. "Behind you!"

Dex turned to find two miners walking toward him, their steps unsteady. Their arms were extended, hands reaching for him. Fingers curved into claws, the nails grown long and caked with dirt.

"The head!" Josh called as he scooted backwards on all fours away from another pack of the miners. "Shoot them in the head!"

Dex ducked beneath the groping hands of the miners and rushed to Josh's side. The wolves growled at the miners, but kept their positions, raising their noses as the smell of death washed over them.

"Did you do this?" Dex asked.

"Not on purpose," Josh said, his voice edged with guilt. "Do you think I'd do this of my own free will?"

Dex pulled Josh to his feet and took his hand. Josh's skin was warm and Dex felt an arc of power jump between them at his touch. "All right, you can raise the dead. Now what?"

Josh turned to frown at him. "What do you mean?"

Dex waved the burning branch at three miners and they shied away from the dancing flame. "Well, can you make them do anything?"

Josh threw his hands up. "How? Ask them?"

"I don't know, try it."

Josh looked at him a moment, brows furrowed, lips tight.

Dex widened his eyes and gestured toward the advancing miners, at least twenty of them. Josh turned, took a breath.

"Stop!"

The miners continued to shuffle toward them. From the corner of his eye, Dex saw the wolves start to move again. The animals were going to flank them, and they would be trapped between the two groups, pinned against the mountain wall.

"It didn't work," Josh said.

"I see that." Dex waved the burning branch at the miners, and they groaned and stepped back, but immediately resumed their relentless advance. "Did you think it as well?"

"What?"

"Put all of your thought into that command," Dex said. "Don't just say it; *think* it at them, too."

"But, Dex—"

"*Do* it!"

Josh turned back to the miners. He clenched his fists and closed his eyes. A moment of silence passed that seemed to stretch to hours as the miners shambled at them and the wolves circled. Dex clenched his teeth as he tried to keep from speaking so as not to interrupt Josh's thoughts. But they were running out of time.

Just as Dex was about to say something, Josh said in a strong, clear voice, "Stop!"

The miners came to a halt, the four in the front staring in gape-mouthed stupor at Josh. Dex swallowed hard and waved the burning branch at the approaching wolves.

Josh blinked and stared at the dead standing before him, waiting for orders. He stepped back into Dex, jumped, and stepped away. The miners groaned and began to move toward them again.

"Stop them again!" Dex shouted and turned in time to see a large wolf rushing at him. "Look out!"

They ducked out of the wolf's path and it landed before the miners. The four men in the front fell on the animal, pinning it to the ground. Their nails dug into the wolf's flesh and the animal snarled and yelped and struggled to get free. More of the miners gathered and laid claim to the wolf. Soon its struggles and cries ceased and the miners tore at the wet, red flesh.

"Jesus," Josh whispered.

"He's got no place here," Dex said. They sat with their backs against the rock wall, the wolves to Dex's right, creeping closer, the miners in front of them, feasting on the wolf. Dex handed Josh the burning branch and reloaded his Colt.

"Listen," Dex said as he took the branch back and jabbed it at a wolf. "When those miners have... finished, try to tell them to attack the wolves."

"What?" Josh looked between the miners and the wolves. "Do you... Do you think they will?"

"It's going to be our only hope," Dex said. "I've got six shots in my gun and there are over a dozen wolves."

As if overhearing their conversation, a few of the miners drifted away from the wolf carcass. In their painful stagger, they moved toward Josh and Dex.

"You can do this, Josh," Dex said. Then he thought, if Josh couldn't do it, they were going to be torn apart by first one group, then the other.

# TWENTY-TWO

Josh took a deep breath and closed his eyes. He focused every thought, every feeling, on the image of the miners attacking the wolves. With that thought firmly in mind, he clenched his fists and *pushed* the image toward the miners, willing it into them.

"It's working," Dex whispered beside him. "They've stopped. They're turning toward the wolves."

Josh kept thinking of the miners engaging in battle with the wolves, feeling the thrum of energy behind the thought. It seemed to flow through his blood, take the heat that had built inside him, twist it into something new and push it out his fingers, leaving his body in waves and cooling him down.

"Keep it up," Dex said. "The wolves are getting nervous and backing away. It's working, Josh! It's working!"

Josh opened his eyes. The miners had abandoned the depleted wolf carcass, turned away from him and Dex, and moved steadily toward the snarling wolves. As the miners shuffled past, Josh counted twenty-five. The stories had always told of 40 miners, and, as he kept the thought of the miners fighting the wolves securely in the front of his mind, he wondered about the location of the rest of the men.

The miners reached the wolves and waded in among them, reaching down to grab handfuls of fur and skin. The wolves growled and jumped, biting at the miners. Their teeth tore the dry, dusty skin and broke apart brittle bones. The first few miners fell and wolves pounced on them. One wolf tore the leg off a miner and trotted out into the dark with the limb dangling from its jaws. More of the miners joined the battle, however, and soon the wolves were overpowered. Several of the animals were gouged as they lay pinned beneath the miners.

"God," Dex said through a wince and turned to Josh with a pained expression. "Are you controlling them now?"

"All I'm doing is imagining them attacking the wolves," Josh replied. "They're just...doing it."

"What happens when they finish with the wolves?" Dex wondered.

"I'll try to tell them to return to the mine, I guess," Josh said.

Dex looked at him a moment, then his gaze shifted to something behind him and his eyes widened. "Josh!"

Something struck the back of Josh's head and he fell forward into blackness.

---

DEX SCRAMBLED TO HIS FEET, aiming his Colt at the girl that crouched beside Josh. It was Laura, one of the girls from the saloon, the one that had attacked him behind the One-Eyed Rooster. Grabbing a fistful of Josh's hair, she lifted his head up and tilted it to the side to expose his throat. She bared fangs that glittered in the moonlight like daggers and paused with her mouth over the steadily pumping side of Josh's neck.

"Get away from him," Dex said. Behind him, the miners shuffled in confusion as what remained of the wolf pack fled into the valley.

"But he smells so delicious," Laura sighed. "And I'm so very hungry."

"Release him or die," Dex said.

Laura lifted her head and grinned. "Your weapon cannot hurt me."

Dex reached into his shirt and pulled out the gold cross. The chain dangled from his fingers, winking in the moonlight as he held the cross out toward her.

"Remember this?"

Laura hissed and leaped back. Josh's head thumped against the rocky cliff wall, the soft, wet sound making Dex flinch. Before Dex could get to him, Josh slumped onto his side, one hand stuck out as though reaching to him, palm up, fingers curled in.

"Stay away from us," Dex shouted. "I know what hurts you."

Laura snapped her fangs at him, crouching a few feet away like a cat. Her eyes gleamed red, the moonlight leaving half her face in shadow.

Dex knelt by Josh and lifted him into his arms. The cross dropped from his fingers and down inside his shirt. In a flash of movement, Laura was beside him. She grabbed Dex by the shoulders and he suddenly felt weightless, flying through the air. He landed hard a dozen feet from Josh, losing his breath.

As he lay gasping for air, Dex fought to stay conscious, to

keep his bearings. He lifted his head, looked back to where he had been kneeling beside Josh, and watched in helpless horror as Laura lifted Josh by the hair to once again expose his throat. She smiled over at Dex, then opened her mouth wide and drew her head back, prepared to bite into Josh's neck.

Shadows moved behind Laura. Shuffling, staggering shadows that reached out to grab her long, dark hair. Laura let out a squawk of surprise. She released her hold on Josh to reach back and disentangle her hair from the miners' fingers.

Dex got to his hands and knees, his lungs slowly remembering their function, and crawled toward Josh. He kept his gaze locked on Laura who knelt right beside Josh, feeling the cross swinging free outside his shirt.

Just as Laura was about to free her hair, one of the miners leaned down and took her fingers in his mouth. He bit down, his teeth cutting easily through skin and bone with a horrendous crackling sound that made Dex shiver as he closed in on Josh.

Laura screamed, the sound echoing off the cliff walls and out into the night, drilling into Dex's head and making him stop to clamp his hands over his ears. The high-pitched, pain-filled shriek drew the rest of the miners and they fell on her. Their teeth tore into Laura's body, ripping skin and breaking bone. A flood of vile, black blood spread across the valley floor, the edge of it reaching out to where Josh lay with his cheek pressed to the sand.

Forcing himself forward, Dex grabbed Josh's hand and dragged him away from the carnage as the miners tore Laura to pieces. Her screams cut off abruptly, and Dex thought he caught a glimpse of a miner lift the glistening mass of her heart, so black in the moonlight, and take a bite from it.

Dex pulled Josh into his arms and patted his cheeks. "Come on, Josh. I need you to wake up. Once these miners are done with her, they're going to come for us."

Josh made no sound, and maybe that was for the best. Dex was glad that Josh would at least not know what was happening when he was torn apart by the miners, but knew he wouldn't be so lucky. He wouldn't make it far carrying Josh into the valley, and the wolf pack was still out there somewhere. All he could do was hunker down and keep them at bay.

He checked to make sure his gun was loaded, and put all but two bullets on the flat surface of a rock by his side. He would save those final two bullets for Josh and himself, if it came down to it. He would not let them be drained of blood by whatever the girls at the Rooster had become, or torn apart by the miners.

As if responding to his thoughts, the miners turned from the pile of limbs, bone, and hair that had been the blood drinking girl. Black blood covered their faces and hands. Their clothes hung in blood-soaked tatters that swung as they stomped and wobbled toward Dex and Josh.

"Aim for the head," Dex whispered and closed one eye. He dropped six of the miners, hitting each in the forehead. His hopes, thin as they were, that the rest might scatter if the first few went down were dashed as the miners behind those stepped on the still forms, heading straight for them.

Dex cursed and opened his Colt, emptying the spent shells and plugging in fresh ones. He reminded himself to save two shots as he slapped the chamber back in place.

One miner in the back of the group staggered and fell. Then a second miner went down, and Dex frowned. What the hell was happening?

Sounds preceded another miner going down. It was the soft whisk of something cutting through the night, followed by the hard impact of the object striking bone. More sounds and more miners collapsed, the limbs of some snapping off. Dex narrowed his eyes and, as he focused on the few remaining miners, saw the glint of moonlight along the shafts of arrows. The arrows came straight down, striking the miners in the tops of the skulls, loosed from the cliffs above.

The final miner jerked under the impact of an arrow, wavered on his feet a moment longer, then fell forward. His hand lay stretched out, bony fingers almost touching Dex's boot.

Dex sat very still, eyes wide and his gaze locked on the miner's bone-white fingers gleaming in the moonlight. As he caught his breath, a trembling started in the center of his chest. It spread down his legs and along his arms until his whole body shuddered. He knew it was reaction to the attacks, but cursed himself for it. Now was not the time for weakness. He needed to protect Josh from whatever would be coming at them next.

The sound of approaching horses pushed Dex into action. He holstered his Colt, picked up Josh, and staggered to his feet. Josh's dead weight pulled on the muscles in Dex's lower back and he shifted his position. Looking around, Dex's gaze landed on the mine entrance and, keeping close to the cliff wall to avoid arrows from above, he started toward it.

Arrows slapped into the dirt several feet in front of him, cutting off his approach to the mine. He stopped and leaned his back against the cliff wall. Josh lay loose limbed in his arms, his weight finally forcing Dex to hunker down and pull Josh against him, wedging the man's body between his legs and wrapping an arm protectively around his chest. Dex drew his Colt and waited.

Moments later, half a dozen horses rounded the bend in the cliff wall and came to a stop before them. Indian braves sat astride the horses, faces pale in the moonlight. The Indians surveyed the bodies strewn about then looked up at Dex.

"Just leave us be," Dex said slowly in a loud, clear voice. "We mean you no harm."

A rider from the back of the group coaxed a horse forward and Dex was surprised to find looking down at him the half-breed girl from the One-Eyed Rooster. She wore a deerskin top and pants and carried a quiver of arrows on her back. Her long, dark hair had been pulled into a single braid that lay down her back.

"I know you," Dex said, relief and exhaustion flooding him.

"Good thing," she replied. "They wanted to kill you along with the miners." She glanced down to Josh. "Was he bitten?"

Dex shook his head. "Out cold. The girl hit the back of his head, but didn't bite him."

She pressed her lips together and nodded. "Good. Let's get him up on a horse."

"Our horses ran out into the valley," Dex said as he got to his feet.

"They caught them a little while ago," the girl said. "They're back at the camp."

Dex helped one of the braves lift Josh onto his horse, then climbed up behind the girl. "I don't know your name."

"Glory."

"Thank you, Glory. I'm Dexter Wells. Dex."

"You're welcome, Dex. Hang onto me; we're going to be riding up some very steep trails."

Dex grabbed Glory tight around the waist and allowed himself to breathe deep and relax as she kicked the horse into a gallop and followed the Indians back the way they had come.

CHAPTER

# TWENTY-THREE

Josh awoke slowly. Pain beat steadily in his head, starting at the back of his skull and branching out fingers around the sides to come together in the middle of his forehead. He could hear quiet conversation and the pop and crackle of a fire. As the pain pulsed inside his head, Josh kept his eyes closed and thought back, trying to figure out where he was.

He could remember the house where he had once lived with his mother. There had been a man, Balthazar, who had called the wolves in to attack the barn. But then Dex had arrived.

*Dex.*

The thought of Dex took the edge off his headache and made him smile.

He and Dex had been together. His cock twitched at the memory and something tightened deep inside his belly. They had been together twice, he remembered now—once at the old house, and another time in Venom Valley.

The memory of the dead miners walking toward them pushed into his mind, followed quickly by the pack of wolves. Josh gasped and chills of terror shook through him. He forced his eyes open and looked at his surroundings.

He was inside a rounded structure, wide at the base and narrow at the top. A small fire burned in a ring of stones directly beneath the opening at the top of the shelter. The walls appeared to be made of animal skins.

The chills of terror returned with the realization he was inside an Indian teepee. He had heard of these, of course. Heard in great detail from the men in town who had raided the nearby Indian camps and come away with furs, animal skins, or, worse, hands strung along a rope.

How had he gotten here? What had happened to the miners and wolves? Where was Dex?

Josh pushed aside the furs that lay atop him and shivered in the chill air. He looked down, surprised to find himself naked except for something on a chain around his neck. Lifting the item, Josh was surprised and concerned to find Dex's gold cross. Where the hell was Dex?

A flap in the side of the teepee pulled back, startling him. He pulled the furs back over himself just before Dex ducked to enter. Dex's face brightened at the sight of Josh sitting up, and he set down the bowl he carried to kneel beside the soft bedding and pull Josh into his arms.

"I'm so glad to see you awake," Dex whispered.

Josh reluctantly pushed back from Dex's embrace, but kept the fingers of one hand entangled with Dex's. "What's happened? Where are we?"

Dex leaned in to kiss him. "Hard to explain. Here, drink this, and I'll tell you."

Dex retrieved the bowl and handed it to him. Josh discovered it was a broth filled with leaves and berries. He sniffed at it, tasted, and decided it was good. As he sipped the broth, Josh listened to Dex relate what had happened up to their arrival at the Indian camp.

"So they're not going to kill us?" Josh asked, glancing around.

Dex shook his head. "No. And Glory's been interpreting for me. They know of Balthazar, have seen him for many years in the woods at night. Several members of their tribe have been taken by him, but they've learned of a few things that can hurt him."

"Oh?"

"Garlic, for one."

"Garlic?" Josh repeated.

Dex nodded and touched the cross that lay on Josh's chest. "And crosses."

"Is that why I'm wearing it?" Josh asked.

Dex smiled. "You've been out a long time. It made me feel better to know you would be safe if you couldn't run." He thought a moment. "Silver seems to cause him pain as well. And they've only seen him at night, so they figure he can't come out in the daylight."

"What about the wolves?" Josh asked. Finished with the broth, he set the bowl aside and lay down again. His headache had dulled but still beat in time with his heart, and lying down made him feel better.

"He seems to be able to control some animals: wolves, bats, snakes."

Josh made a face. "Creatures of the night."

"Pretty much. Also, he can bewitch you if you look into his eyes too long."

Josh widened his eyes. "He tried to do that to me."

Dex nodded. "That's what I thought. They know he drinks blood and, if he bites a person three times, they will change into a vampire like him."

"Vampire?" Josh repeated.

"That's what Glory said he told her he was. He said he came from across the sea years ago. Banished, I think was the word she used." Dex leaned down to rest a palm against Josh's cheek. "Anyway, that's enough talk of vampires."

Josh leaned into Dex's palm, felt the comforting warmth as he looked up into the familiar blue eyes. "What else is there to talk about?"

"The miners, for one," Dex said.

Josh shuddered and looked away. "I don't want to talk about them."

"The vampire girl had knocked you out and the miners turned on us. But then they attacked her. They..." Dex paused and his eyes darted away a moment, a haunted expression drifting across his handsome face. "They bit her. Bit *into* her. Their teeth could penetrate her skin and break her bones." Dex leaned down to kiss Josh's forehead. As he moved away, his hand touched the fur covering and he raised an eyebrow. "Is it warm under there?"

Josh smiled and nodded. "It is."

Dex glanced at the flap hiding the entrance to the teepee, then back at Josh. "Is there room for one more?"

Josh stuck his tongue out of the corner of his mouth and pretended to search around beneath the furs. "I think so, yes."

Dex grinned. He stood up to undress, ducking his head to avoid hitting it on the side of the teepee. With his clothes in a pile, Dex stood naked above Josh a moment. His cock lay half hard along his left thigh and he stroked it, his gaze locked on Josh's face.

A response to the sight of Dex standing above him was swift, and Josh was hard in a moment. He licked his lips as he moved over on the padded sleeping space and Dex slid beneath the furs. The feel of Dex, the heated touch of Dex's sweat-sticky skin against his, the brush of his body hair, the smell of him, almost pushed Josh to climax right away. He closed his eyes and willed himself to a calm place.

"Hey," Dex whispered. "Where'd you go?"

Josh opened his eyes and smiled as he blushed. "I had to think of something else for a minute."

Dex grinned. "Truth?"

Josh grinned back. "Truth."

They kissed. Dex's mouth tasted like the broth Josh had eaten. The slow, easy curl of Dex's tongue into his mouth sent pricklings of excitement rushing across Josh's skin. Dex eased over on top of him, his broad, hairy chest feeling so good, so right, against Josh's own smooth skin. He could feel the stubborn hardness of Dex's cock alongside his own, feel the tacky-slick fluid that seeped from the tip.

"I love you," Dex whispered into his mouth. "I've loved you for so many years."

"I love you, too," Josh replied.

Dex surprised him by sliding beneath the fur coverings, and Josh sighed and moaned as Dex moved down his body, pausing now and then to brush his lips over skin. Dex grabbed the root of Josh's throbbing cock and slowly stroked it. Josh groaned quietly and writhed beneath him. Dex ran the wet, hot width of his tongue from the base to the tip, then took the full length in his mouth.

Josh gasped and a gurgle of surprise bubbled out of his throat. He remembered they were behind very thin walls, and pressed his lips together as Dex sucked him, his head a bobbing lump beneath the furs. Josh closed his eyes and grabbed fistfuls of the wrappings beneath him. His focus, his world, narrowed to the feeling of his cock in Dex's mouth, and in a matter of seconds he lost all sense of place and time. His cock jumped and, with a quiet grunting, he came hard. Dex swallowed all that Josh provided, lips pressed tight around his fevered shaft.

After running his tongue around the sensitive and swollen tip to clean it, Dex moved up Josh's body. He kissed and licked each nipple before pushing his head out from beneath the furs. Sweat plastered his hair to his head and his face was flushed pink and shiny.

"You're overheated," Josh said as he kissed his swollen lips.

"I'm happy," Dex replied.

Josh grinned and pushed him onto his back. "Not quite yet."

He kissed Dex again on the lips, darting his tongue between them and tasting himself. Moving lower, Josh ducked beneath the furs and was surprised at the damp heat beneath. He smelled the tang of Dex's sweat and ran his tongue along the man's skin, tasting the salt. He kissed and sucked the hard points of his nipples rising through the fine dark hairs on his chest. The hard spike of Dex's cock throbbed impatiently against Josh's chest as he slid lower, and Dex sighed and groaned, his hips lifting and thrusting beneath him.

Sweat stung Josh's eyes as he finally came to a stop with Dex's cock resting along his cheek. He felt the wet slap of it on his whiskered jaw, and the sticky patch of slick left behind. He copied the motions Dex had used on him, running his tongue from the spot at the base where it joined with Dex's balls and up the heated length to the shrouded tip. Josh eased the foreskin down to expose the fat, slick tip and swirled his tongue around it before lowering his mouth.

"Oh, God," Dex gasped. "Josh."

Josh held the sound of his name whispered on Dex's lips in his chest as he sucked Dex's cock. The gold cross Dex had left around his neck for protection swung back and forth between them. Sweat ran down the side of Josh's face and stood out on his back and his legs as he worked Dex's cock. He was about to pause for a breath when he felt Dex's leg muscles tighten beneath him. Josh increased his speed, one hand stroking in time with his mouth while the other cupped Dex's balls.

Semen burst into his mouth and Josh hungrily gulped it down. This was the very essence of Dex, the part of him no other knew. This part of him was for Josh alone, and he savored the thick, spicy taste.

He nursed on Dex's softening cock before sliding out from beneath the furs to draw in a great breath of fresh air. Dex smiled and kissed him hard.

"I love you," Dex said.

Josh grinned. "You said that."

Another kiss. "You deserve to hear it again. There were so many times over the years I've wanted to say it to you, I want to take every opportunity to tell you now."

Josh put his head on Dex's chest. "What time of day it is?"

Dex kissed the top of his head. "You slept through a day."

Josh lifted his head quickly, wincing at the sudden sweep of pain at the back of his skull, and widened his eyes. "I slept a whole day?"

Dex nodded. "You slept through the night and then the entire next day. The sun set not more than an hour ago."

Josh sighed and rubbed his eyes. "We lost a day?"

"She hit you on the head pretty hard." Dex kissed his forehead, then the side of his head. "You need to rest."

"How can we rest when there's so much to do?" Josh asked.

Dex frowned at him. "What do you think we need to do?"

"Find Balthazar," Josh said. "We know how to hurt him. And if we don't stop him, he'll turn everyone in Belkin's Pass into vampires like him. If he hasn't already."

"We have time," Dex said and kissed him on the mouth. "Even heroes need some time to rest."

"Well, let's not forget that I've got a bounty on my head. And I'm sure you do now as well."

"And who is going to look for us in an Indian camp above Venom Valley?" Dex leaned in for another kiss, then stopped.

Josh looked at him, his brows drawn together. "What is it?"

"I thought I heard something." Dex turned his head to peer at the teepee flap, listening, and Josh held his breath. It was quiet outside the animal skin walls, too quiet. Before there had been quiet conversations and movement, but now that had all ceased.

Dex leaned down to put his lips against Josh's ear. The brush of Dex's whiskers sent a shiver of attraction through him that quickly died away when Dex whispered, "Get dressed."

They slipped out from beneath the furs and pulled on their clothes. Josh looked around for his rifle but it wasn't there. Dex crouched by the flap, looking outside. Josh hunkered down behind him, hands on Dex's back. A feeling of finality fluttered inside his chest, spreading a sense of unease. He wanted nothing more than to turn around, undress, and get back beneath the fur coverings. Hadn't Dex just said even heroes deserved a day of rest?

"Is it safe?" Josh whispered.

"Only one way to find out," Dex replied and turned to give him a tight smile. "Ready?"

Josh swallowed and nodded. He followed Dex out of the teepee and they turned toward the large fire blazing in the center of the camp. Fear jumped in Josh's chest at the sight of the Indian men and women standing on the other side of the fire, eyes wide in the firelight as they stared at them. Had the tribe heard them being intimate and found it an offense?

Movement beside him caused Josh to turn toward Dex, but he was no longer there. Josh turned to look farther back in the darkness toward the woods and icy dread shot through him.

Balthazar stood on the edge of the firelight. He grinned wickedly at Josh, his eyes gleaming red beneath the shadow of his heavy brow. Balthazar held Dex tight against him, one hand on his throat, ready to crush his airway, the other gripped his chest, holding Dex in front of him as a shield.

"Let him go!" Josh shouted and started forward. The Indians shouted behind him and over their foreign words he could hear a woman shouting at him in English to stop.

"Don't come any closer or I'll kill him," Balthazar said, his voice calm. He tightened his grip around Dex's throat and Dex's eyes bulged. His face turned red and he struggled for breath. "It would be so easy."

Josh stopped in his tracks, fists clenched at his sides. He took deep breaths as he tried to think of something, anything, he could do to save Dex. He remembered he wore Dex's cross and held it up.

Balthazar flinched and turned away in distaste. "Put that away."

"It hurts you," Josh noted.

"Not as much as it would hurt you for me to kill him here in front of you," Balthazar said and turned back to glare at Josh. "Put. It. Away."

Josh swallowed his fear as he tucked the cross back inside his shirt. "What do you want?"

"We need to feed." Balthazar glanced over his shoulder and two pale, beautiful women materialized out of the shadows.

Josh heard a gasp and someone approached from behind him. He turned to find standing beside him the half-breed girl from the One-Eyed Rooster who Dex had told him was named Glory. Her shadowed face was tight with tension, but a warm, golden glow seemed to surround her, apart from the yellow light of the fire. Josh caught a glimpse of what looked like an Indian brave standing on her other side, but each time he tried to look directly at him, the Indian vanished.

"Edith? Hazel?" Glory said. "Oh my God. Edith, what has he done to you?"

One of the girls, Josh presumed it was Edith, smiled, showing her fangs, and walked toward them. Josh held up his cross and Glory held out cloves of garlic laced together with rawhide. Edith hissed and, holding up a hand, backed off. The other girl, Hazel, hissed as well.

Balthazar sneered at them. "Do you think garlic and a tiny cross can keep us from taking all of you if we wanted?"

"Let him go," Glory said. Josh saw tears running down her cheeks. "You've got Edith and Hazel. Take them, leave him, and we'll leave you to your damned life in the valley."

Balthazar cocked an eyebrow at her. "Do you haggle with me over this man's life?"

Josh stared at Dex, holding his gaze, trying to will him strength for escape. Each time Dex moved, though, Balthazar's grip tightened on his throat and he was forced to stop. How could this be happening? Hadn't they been through enough? Dex stared at him, into him, and mouthed the words *I love you.*

Something buzzed past Josh's ear, flying through the space between himself and Glory. Hazel shrieked as the arrow lodged deep in her chest, directly over her heart.

"Hazel!" Glory shouted and rushed forward.

Balthazar and Edith looked down as Hazel crumpled to the ground at their feet. Balthazar threw back his head and let out a horrifying scream of anger and pain, then leveled a hateful glare at Josh.

"You took someone from me," Balthazar said. "And now I take someone from you."

In a blur of motion, Balthazar was gone, taking Dex with him.

"No!" Josh screamed and ran forward. He stopped beside Glory who knelt in the circle of firelight holding Hazel. Edith stood for a moment on the edge of the firelight, a dozen feet away, watching Glory.

"Glory," Edith said, her red eyes almost sad.

"Oh, Edith," Glory said as tears ran down her face. "Don't give in. Remember who you are."

"You knew who I was, Glory. That Edith is no more." A flicker of movement and she was gone.

Josh stood and stared into the dark woods, looking for any sign of them. It was too late. Balthazar was gone and he had taken Dex. His chest felt cold, empty, as though a deep space inside had opened up and consumed his heart. Dex was gone.

"Oh, Hazel," Glory whispered, drawing Josh's attention.

Hazel vomited black, vile smelling blood and her hands and feet pounded against the ground. She turned her eyes up to Glory's face and, for a quick moment, Josh thought the girl smiled. Then Hazel's eyes went blank and her face turned gray. Her skin changed to something that reminded Josh of the paper wasp nests he used to have to knock down from the eaves of the schoolhouse for Agnes. The night breeze took the ash of Hazel's body and scattered it into the woods, leaving only her clothes and the wooden shaft of the arrow.

Glory held the arrow in her palms. The point gleamed in the firelight and Josh thought it looked to be made of silver.

"She was a good soul," Glory said. She stood and turned to face the tribe who still stood on the other side of the fire. "Who did this? Who killed her?" She stomped back to the fire and brandished the arrow at each Indian brave, demanding to know who shot Hazel. No one spoke and, finally, Glory fell to her knees by the fire and wept into her hands.

Josh turned away from the tribe as tears filled his eyes. He held Dex's cross in his fist and looked up at the stars so bright overhead.

"I will come for you, Dex," Josh whispered to the night sky. "I promise you."

# TWENTY-FOUR

The morning sun was bright and Josh had difficulty putting the events of the night in context with the calm, sunny day. Had it actually happened? Had he stood by helplessly and watched Dex get carried away by Balthazar? What suffering had Dex been subjected to all night?

He packed the last bit of food provided by the Indians and turned to look for Glory. The teepee where he and Dex had lain together caught his eye and Josh paused, reaching up to touch Dex's gold cross hanging beneath his shirt. A chill wind tousled his hair and Josh blinked, then looked to where Glory stood talking with the tribe's chief.

"We need to go, Glory," he called and climbed up into Clementine's saddle.

He didn't understand how he knew it, but he felt Dex was still alive. And if Dex was still alive, Josh was going to do everything he could to save him. It was what Dex would do for him.

But he was afraid they didn't have much time.

Clementine snorted and pawed at the ground as if eager to be off. Nightshade stood alongside Clem, snorting and tossing his head as well.

As Glory approached, an old squaw, her gray hair done in two long braids and her brown face round and wrinkled, stepped up to her. Josh watched as the old woman said a few things he couldn't understand, but from her expression and the sharp motions she made with her hands, they weren't kind. Glory said something short in reply, turned, and continued on her path to the horses, her expression sad and angry.

"What was that about?" Josh asked.

Glory shook her head. "It was nothing. She is the elder mother of the camp, and she wanted to let me know I am not full-blooded Apache."

"That's it?"

Glory took a breath and looked up at him, forcing a smile. "The chief wished us a safe journey. They say Balthazar most likely inhabits a series of caves by the narrow pass at the end of Venom Valley."

She mounted Nightshade and looked over at Josh. "We may not make it there before nightfall. Are you sure you want to ride through the valley?"

Josh nodded and turned in his saddle to face the tribal chief. He held his fist over his heart and lowered his head in respect. The chief bowed his head in return and said something in his deep, smooth voice. Josh turned to look at Glory.

"He said your path will change," she translated, "but remain true to your quest."

Josh looked around the camp once more, taking in the faces of the braves and squaws, the children holding onto their mothers' hands. He noted the old woman, the elder mother who had spoken with Glory, standing back from the rest of the tribe. Her eyes were narrowed and her fists clenched as she stared right back. Josh turned away with a shiver, glad to put the old woman's cold stare behind him, and then he turned Clementine toward the path through the woods.

"Let's go," he called over his shoulder. "We're losing light."

"Are you sure you know what you're doing?" Glory shouted to him as the horses pounded along the path. "What about Belkin's Pass? We could go back to town and get some reinforcements."

"No," Josh said. "I have a bounty on my head. And, besides, from what you and Dex said, Balthazar's been feeding there. Belkin's Pass is lost."

"But, we could try to help them," Glory protested. "They're our friends, our family."

Josh reined Clementine to a stop and glared at her. "They were nothing but cruel to you, why do you want to go back for them?"

Glory's eyes flashed with anger. "Not all of them were cruel to me, some were kind. And they don't deserve to end up like...like Edith."

"No," Josh said again. "We ride to the end of Venom Valley. Dex doesn't have a lot of time." He turned away and kicked Clementine to a fast run.

"Balthazar's probably got an army of vampires now," Glory shouted at his back. "How do you plan to fight 'em?"

Josh smiled grimly as he ducked beneath a branch. "I've got a few surprises for Balthazar."

"Care to share them with me?"

"In time," Josh said, and looked out over the edge of the

cliff to where Venom Valley stretched out toward the foot of the mountains. "In time."

———

To be continued in
## STAKES & SPURS: VENOM VALLEY
## BOOK TWO

# STAKES & SPURS: VENOM VALLEY BOOK TWO

*New lovers torn apart.*
*An ancient evil consuming a small town.*
*Unlikely heroes running out of time.*

Dex Wells, former deputy of the prairie town of Belkin's Pass, has been taken captive by the wicked vampire Balthazar and held in the caves above Venom Valley. He knows he is being kept as bait, a way to lure Dex's lover, Josh, into the caves in order to capture him. As Dex tries to escape, he realizes he's not the only prisoner Balthazar keeps chained in those dark depths.

Josh Stanton can raise the dead. It's a power he's always had within him but never understood. Now, he's trying to become more skilled at wielding that power, and using it to battle Balthazar and rescue Dex. But there's still a bounty on Josh's head for a murder he did not commit, and he ends up back in Belkin's Pass with Glory, a half White, half Apache former saloon girl watched over by a Native American spirit.

Two members of the US Army arrive and, with no lawmen left in town, take Josh into custody. It's up to Josh and Glory to convince these men the truth about their small town and find a way to save Dex before Balthazar turns him into a vampire as well.

Grab your copy today: https://books2read.com/stakesandspurs/

# ABOUT THE AUTHOR

Hank Edwards (he/him) has been writing gay fiction for more than twenty years. He has published over forty novels and novellas and dozens of short stories. His writing crosses many sub-genres, including contemporary romance, rom-com, paranormal, suspense, mystery, wacky comedy, and erotica. He has written a number of series such as the funny and spooky Critter Catchers, Old West historical horror of Venom Valley, suspenseful FBI and civilian Up to Trouble, and the erotic and funny Fluffers, Inc. Under the pen name R. G. Thomas, he has written a young adult urban fantasy gay romance series called The Town of Superstition. He was born and still lives in a northwest suburb of the Motor City, Detroit, Michigan.

For more information:
www.hankedwardsbooks.com
hankedwardsbooks@gmail.com
www.facebook.com/groups/hankshangout

# ALSO BY HANK EDWARDS

**<u>Critter Catchers Series</u>**

Terror by Moonlight

Chasing the Chupacabra

Swamped by Fear

The Devil of Pinesville

Screams of the Season

Horror at Hideaway Cove

Dread of Night

Critter Catchers Box Set 1

Critter Catchers Box Set 2

**<u>Critter Catchers Universe Stories</u>**

The Mystery of the Morelock Motel

**<u>Critter Catchers: Level Up Series</u>**

Grave Danger

Wet Screams

**<u>Williamsville Inn Gay Romance:</u>**

Snowflakes and Song Lyrics

The Cupid Crawl

Fake Date Flip-Flop

Star-Spangled Showdown

**<u>Lacetown Murder Mysteries</u>**

**(co-written with Deanna Wadsworth)**

Murder Most Lovely

Murder Most Deserving

**<u>Venom Valley Series</u>**

Cowboys & Vampires

Stakes & Spurs

Blood & Stone

**<u>Up to Trouble Series</u>**

Holed Up

Shacked Up

Roughed Up

Choked Up

**<u>Fluffers, Inc. Series</u>**

Fluffers, Inc.

A Carnal Cruise

Vancouver Nights

**<u>Standalone Gay Romance</u>**

Buried Secrets

Destiny's Bastard

Hired Muscle

Plus Ones

Repossession is 9/10ths of the Law

Wicked Reflection

## **Holiday Gay Romance:**

A Gift for Greg (A Story Orgy Single)

Mistletoe at Midnight (A Story Orgy Single)

The Christmas Accomplice

## **Story Orgy Singles Gay Romance:**

A Gift for Greg

By the Book

Cross Country Foreplay

Mistletoe at Midnight

The Cheapskate: Bad Boyfriends

With This Ring

The Story Orgy Singles Boxed Set

## **The Town of Superstition (YA urban fantasy series)**
## **Published under pen name R. G. Thomas**

The Midnight Gardener

The Well of Tears

The Battle of Iron Gulch

A Tangle of Secrets

## **Gay Erotic Short Story Collections:**

A Very Dirty Dozen

Another Very Dirty Dozen

A Third Very Dirty Dozen

A Fourth Very Dirty Dozen

**<u>Salacious Singles Gay Erotic Short Stories</u>**:

Bear Market

Convoy

Double Down

Exchange Rate

Finding North

Hotel Dick

Kindred Spirits

Sacked

Stroking Midnight

Vanity Loves Company

Wet Lands